Praise for Telling

this frank, yet sensitive portrayal of child molestation, Reynolds
s done a superb job of weaving the comple~··· ·ficult issues
o the life of an innocent child. Th~   evable and
mpathetic, especially Cassie ¿   Her story
sonates with authenticity, and   eaders.

                                                  ..¡ y Journal

n-sensational yet specific, thi·   .·ıtten book explores the
nflicting emotions of both an early adolescent who cannot fathom
·y an adult male would find her attractive and parents who must
·e the difficulty of protecting their daughter while exposing a
ngerous individual. A sad, frightening, ultimately hopeful, and
finitely worthwhile purchase.

—*Booklist*

e of the most realistic accounts available of the dilemma posed by
·ual abuse of a minor is presented in this fine true-life story which
·onicles a young pre-teen's confusion when an admired neighbor
·roaches her.   —*Midwest Book Review*

and Readers Say...

·ave been through sexual abuse with my stepfather and your book
·ut telling just helped me realize that I had to tell what happened.

—C.G.

·nk you for writing this book. I simply wish I would have read it
·lier so when I was a victim, I would have known what to do. Your
·k spoke to me. I find out on August 31 what sentence my assaulter
· face. That day, I will be free from the chains he attached to me
·ong ago.   —A.R.

·ow that if I would have seen this book when I was eleven, when
· same thing was happening to me, I might have had the courage
·ell someone before it went too far. Your book gives a helping hand
·all the hurting girls out there. . .and helps parents confront this
·ıe to help the daughters get through their ordeals.

—N.M.

The Complete True-to-Life Series
from Hamilton High

Also available as e-books

1
2/23

Telling

By Marilyn Reynolds

For Béa & Elena —
Remember the importance of
Telling!
Marilyn Reynolds

NEW WIND
PUBLISHING

Sacramento, California

New Wind Publishing
Copyright 1996, 2012, 2014 Marilyn Reynolds

All Rights Reserved

No part of this publication may be adapted, reproduced, stored in a
retrieval system, or transmitted in any form or by any means, electronic,
mechanical, photocopying, recording, or otherwise without permission
from the publisher. Like Marilyn Reynolds' other novels, Telling is part
of the True-to-Life Series from Hamilton High, a fictional, urban, ethni-
cally mixed high school somewhere in Southern California. Characters
in the stories are imaginary and do not represent actual people or places.

Originally published by Peace Ventures Press in 1989 and Morning
Glory Press in 1996.

Library of Congress Cataloging-in-Publication Data

Reynolds, Marilyn, 1935-
  Telling / by Marilyn Reynolds.
Summary: After being sexually abused by the father of the children she
is babysitting, twelve-year-old Cassie faces a difficult journey before she
finds the strength and insight to deal with the problem.

ISBN 978-1-929777-08-2
  1. Child sexual abuse—Fiction. 2. Title. 3. Series: Reynolds, Marilyn,
1935- True-to-life series from Hamilton High.
PZ7.R3373Te 1996
95-39149
[Fic]--dc20

New Wind Publishing
Sacramento, California, 95819
www.newwindpublishing.com

I was at the Sloanes' house, waiting for them to leave for the movie. Fred walked in and I thought he was going to make a joke or something because he had this strange look on his face. He walked right up to where I was standing, and then he grabbed me with both hands, pulling me hard against his body.

I tried to back away from him, with my fists pushing at his stomach, but he was so strong, holding me so close, that I couldn't even move ...

To Century High School students, past and present.
They also teach.

ACKNOWLEDGMENTS

To Gloria D. Miklowitz for encouraging me to write this story somewhere back around 1987, and to Peace Ventures Press for believing in it from the beginning, I am particularly grateful.

For the opportunity to keep Cassie's story alive as part of the True-to-Life Series, I thank Jeanne Lindsay of Morning Glory Press.

I thank the readers who write or email to tell me how important this story has been in their lives. Their letters touch me beyond words.

A special thanks goes to Terry Ahrens and Cathryne Ahrens, whose work has been instrumental in keeping *Telling* in print.

Thanks also to Subei Reynolds Kyle for her insights and close reading of this manuscript.

Marilyn Reynolds

CHAPTER

1

My little brother, Robbie, made a flying leap onto my bed. I knew my Saturday morning sleep was over, even though I kept my eyes closed very tightly, hoping Robbie would disappear.

"Get up, Cassie," he begged, trying to open my eyes with his jelly-sticky fingers.

"MOM!" I yelled. "Can't you make Robbie stay out of my room?"

"It's time for you to get up anyway," Mom yelled back from the kitchen. "I need you to help clean up around here."

I groaned and turned over on my stomach. Robbie straddled my back and bounced. "Giddy-up, Horsie," he giggled.

"Get out, Brat"

"MOM! CASSIE CALLED ME BRAT AGAIN!"

Mom stomped down the hall and filled my doorway with her worst frown. "I told you not to call him that, Cassie. It's not good for his self-image. Now get up and make yourself useful around here."

Well, that's the way it always goes. Robbie acts stupid and I get in trouble. Just because I'm twelve and he's only five, he can get away with everything and I'm supposed to be perfect.

As soon as Mom went back down the hallway, Robbie started chanting, "I know something you don't know," over and over again.

"Do not," I said.

"Do too," Robbie answered.

"Not."

"Too."

"Not."

"Too."

I rolled over and looked at him. He had the grin he gets when he really does know something.

"So what is it?"

Last year, in English, we talked about the inner conflicts of characters in literature. I'd never thought that much about inner conflict before, but now I could see evidence of it on Robbie's face. He wanted to keep a secret because it made him feel big, but he's the kind of kid who also wants to tell everything he knows. I grabbed a foot and started tickling. He squirmed and squealed and agreed to tell.

"You know the house where the mean lady used to live, where the weeds are all grown up?"

I nodded.

"Now Tina and Dorian live there," he said. His blue eyes sparkled with the news.

"So who are Tina and Dorian?"

"Tina's three and Dorian's five. When school starts he can ride with us."

"Are there any kids my age?"

"Nope. But there's a dog, Smiley, and two goldfish, Swimmy and Floaty."

"When did you meet them?"

"Just this morning. When they were emptying the moving van. Dorian gave me a donut but it was Tina's so she cried but his mom gave Tina her donut so it was okay and they liked me. The dad has a great big motorcycle, too, and a helmet."

Even if he always gets me in trouble, I still like Robbie. In fact, he cracks me up. This family lives in our neighborhood for about half an hour and he already knows all about them. At least that's what I thought then. Now I realize there was a lot about the Sloane family that we had yet to learn.

It was afternoon by the time we finished emptying all the trash, vacuuming the whole house, and folding the laundry.

Telling

"Thanks for the help," Mom told me, as if I'd had some choice in the matter.

My dad came in all dirty and sweaty from raking the leaves out back.

"Let's call it quits for the day, Helen," he said to Mom. "The new Michael Caine movie is at the Cineplex. We could take in a matinee."

Mom looked around the kitchen. "I don't know, Les."

"Let's live a little," Dad smiled. "I'll take you out for ice cream after the show."

So that's what they did, and I got stuck with Robbie. But it was okay. My friend Mandy and I usually go together on Saturday afternoons, and then spend the night together, too. But this weekend Mandy was visiting her father out in the desert, so I didn't have anything else to do anyway.

After my folks left, Robbie went over to the new neighbors to play with Dorian. He'd been gone an hour when I decided to check on him.

I walked through knee-high weeds to the front door and called, "Robbie. Robbie."

A woman who looked more like a teenager opened the door. She was wearing jeans and a very large sweatshirt with rolled-up sleeves.

"You must be Cassie Jenkins," she said, smiling and showing perfectly white movie star teeth. "I'm Angie Sloane. Robbie's told us a lot about you. Come in."

I stepped over a box of toys blocking the doorway and saw Robbie and his new friend sitting on the floor with about a hundred little cars strung out all around them. Each boy gripped an oozing peanut butter and jelly sandwich. The room was cluttered with unpacked boxes.

"What a mess, huh? But our refrigerator's hooked up. Can I get you a cold soda?"

"No, thank you, Mrs. Sloane," I said.

"Oh, just call me Angie. I have a feeling we'll be seeing a lot of each other, so let's not be too formal. Do you ever babysit?"

"Sometimes," I said. Really, I didn't babysit for anyone but Robbie, but I wanted to because I wanted to start making my own money.

I couldn't stop looking at Angie. She didn't look like a mother at all. She was thin but healthy looking, and she had reddish hair that bounced lightly at her shoulder, the way the TV shampoo ads always made me hope mine would.

A man came walking into the living room carrying a small table and lamp.

"Where do you want this, Babe?" he said to Angie, then turned to me.

"I'll bet you're Cassie," he said, smiling. "We're all enjoying your brother's company."

I could tell big mouth Robbie had told everything he knew about me, and had probably even made stuff up. He loved to make up stories and pretend they were true.

"This is Fred. He's the man of the house," Angie said, laughing.

Fred was about a head taller than Angie. He had curly, sandy-colored hair. His T-shirt was damp with sweat, and his arms were tanned and muscular.

It all seemed natural, that I would stay and help entertain kids while Angie and Fred worked at putting things away, and that later when Fred ordered pizza there would be plenty for me and Robbie, and we would stay and eat with them, as if we'd always known them.

After dinner, while Fred worked putting up shelves in the garage, Angie and I lined the kitchen cupboards with paper and put away dishes and glasses, pots and pans. As we worked she told me of their plans for the house, which they could only afford because it needed so much work.

"I know we'll miss my parents in Minnesota," she told me. "But we wanted to raise Dorian and Tina in a place that's warm and free. And Fred wanted to start fresh somewhere, too. And look at you and Robbie," she smiled. "I feel as if we've already found family here in California."

I took Robbie home from the Sloanes' about nine that evening, with promises to return the next day. He was so tired from playing all day with Dorian and Tina that he went straight to bed with no argument. That was rare for Robbie.

"Tell us about our new neighbors," Daddy said.

I told them how nice the Sloanes were, and how young, and how messed up their house was. But it was a mistake to tell them how I'd helped Angie in the kitchen because Mom decided it was time for us to put in new shelf paper.

"Now that you have some experience lining shelves, you won't mind helping me do the same thing next Saturday."

I hoped she'd forget by next Saturday. I don't know why, but working at the Sloanes' had been fun. Working at home was boring.

Sunday I went back to the Sloanes after breakfast. I hadn't planned to stay long, but they were painting Tina's room and Fred handed me a brush.

"You're lower to the floor than we are," he said. "How about painting the baseboard?"

After I did that, I painted some shelves white and I also painted Tina's little baby rocking chair. It was finished by afternoon, and it looked great. While Fred and I admired our work, Angie brought in a beer for each of them and a soda for me, and a big basket of chips.

"Do you play cards, Cassie?" Fred asked.

"Some," I said.

"Gin Rummy? Hearts?"

I shook my head. I was embarrassed to say that I mostly just played Fish and Old Maid with Robbie.

"We'll teach you," he said.

Angie smiled. "I have a feeling that card playing is going to be our major entertainment for a while. I don't think we're going to be spending a lot of money on fancy dinners and nightclubs."

So that's how it went that summer. Almost every day I went over to the Sloanes' and helped Angie with some project—scraping old paint off windowsills or pulling tattered wallpaper off the dining room walls. Sometimes my friend Mandy would come over with me, but during August she stayed a lot of the time with her dad so it was mostly just me. About twice a week Angie would call Fred at work at lunchtime and tell him, "Cassie and I are tired of this working around the house business. We're taking the kids to the beach."

We'd pack a bunch of sandwiches and soft drinks and towels, and I'd call my mom at work so she wouldn't be worried, and off we'd go. The funny thing was that I felt like a grown-up with Angie and she said she felt like a kid with me.

Almost every Tuesday night Angie and Fred and I would play Hearts. I got to be pretty good. On Saturday nights I usually babysat for Tina and Dorian while Angie and Fred went out to a movie or something. I saved my babysitting money for school clothes because I wanted to look right when I started Palm Avenue Junior High School. But I didn't tell my mom I was saving money. I wanted to get all I could from her first, and then get extra stuff with my own money.

Sometimes my mom would get mad at me and say, "You practically live with Fred and Angie. I think you like them better than your own family."

When she said that, I knew she wanted me to say back to her that I liked my family best of all. But I couldn't. For a while I did like the Sloanes best. I felt important and older with them, and appreciated. They laughed at my jokes and they asked what I thought about stuff. They treated me almost like an equal, and at home I still felt like a little kid.

In September, when school started, the Tuesday night card games stopped because my parents wouldn't let me go out on weeknights. And of course the trips to the beach stopped, too. I had a lot of homework, and Mandy and I were both on the soccer team, and we had to practice a lot after school. But I still saw the Sloanes on weekends, and we were still almost like best friends—until that night in January, when everything changed.

CHAPTER

2

It was just after New Year's. I was at the Sloanes' house, standing in the living room, waiting for them to leave for the movie. Angie was in the bedroom getting dressed. Tina and Dorian were watching TV in the den. Fred walked into the living room. I thought he was going to make a joke or something. He had this strange look on his face. He walked right up to where I was standing, and then he grabbed me with both hands, pulling me hard against his body.

I tried to back away from him, with my fists pushing at his stomach, but he was so strong, holding me so close, that I couldn't even move. He forced my head back with his chin. His mouth was so tight against mine and his tongue was strong, pushing into my mouth. Then, as quickly as he had grabbed me, he let go and turned away from me. In the next instant, Angie came into the room.

"We'd better go, Fred, if we're going to catch the beginning of the movie."

"Sure, Babe. Just waitin' on you," he said with a grin, glancing over at me. "Huh, Cassie? Just waitin' around. Waitin' around."

Angie laughed. "It's about time you waited for me for a change—I wait on you all the time." Then she told me, "The kids are bathed and fed. All you need to do is get them to bed. Try for around 8:30." She looked at me then, really for the first time since she'd walked into the room. "Are you okay, Cassie? You look a bit flushed."

"I'm fine," I mumbled.

"We should be back by 10:00—right Fred?"

"Yep, unless we decide to park on a dark street for a while before I bring you home," Fred said, winking at me as he opened the front door for Angie. I watched them out the window as they walked to their car. Fred had his arm around Angie and they were laughing. They were both wearing jeans, kind of tight, and they really did look like something you might see on a commercial. They seemed a lot younger and more "with it" than my parents. But watching them out that window, was I ever mixed up! I mean, they looked happy, and like they were still even in love, and Fred, the same guy who was now opening the door for Angie, had just a few minutes ago been doing this movie style kissing on my mouth. Everything seemed strange to me, like I was in a daze or something. I think I went kind of numb.

I watched the Sloanes' green Toyota van as it turned the corner. Then I went into the bathroom to wash my face. Tina, the three-year-old, was right behind me, pulling at my pant leg. I soaped up my face and scrubbed hard with warm water, all the time with Tina pulling at me and yelling, "Cassie, Cassie! Play the game with us, Cassie! Play the game." Then Dorian came in and started pulling at me, too.

"Yeah, Cassie! The game! The game!"

I didn't feel like playing with them at all, but I didn't feel like listening to them beg, either. I picked Tina up and carried her to the den, with Dorian running along beside me. I dumped Tina on the big couch and began the expected, traditional, belly button search. I was just going through the motions to quiet Tina and Dorian. Pretty soon though, I lost some of my numbness and began to give it some enthusiasm. I sat on the couch next to Tina and put her on my lap.

"Poor Tina. Poor, poor Tina," I said, pretending to cry. Then I told Dorian in a loud whisper, "Dorian! Help! Something terrible has happened! Tina's lost her belly button!"

"No!" Dorian screeched. "Look at her tummy, Cassie!"

Tina giggled and squirmed while I checked each of her

toes. Dorian pulled up Tina's pajama top. "Look, Cassie! It's right here!"

"Well, I'll be ... It's a belly button all right. But can't you see? That's another belly button. That's not Tina's. Oh, this is awful!"

We carried on like this for what seemed like forever. Then finally, predictably, I let myself be convinced that all belly buttons were in their rightful places, and the three of us settled into the big, pillowy couch to watch TV.

The belly button search had been a distraction, but as soon as things were quiet, the numbness began to creep over me again.

After the bedtime stories and trips to the bathroom and drinks of water and more trips to the bathroom, when Tina and Dorian were finally in bed, I went back to the den to watch "MASH" re-runs and diagram sentences. But I couldn't concentrate. I kept feeling Fred's body against mine, his tongue pushing at my mouth. It's not that I kept thinking about it—I just kept feeling it. My face felt hot, and my mouth felt dirty. I went into the bathroom and splashed cold water on my cheeks and forehead. I washed my face again and rinsed my mouth out, over and over. I looked in the mirror for a long time. Big nose. Thick eyebrows. Dull brown hair. Dull brown eyes. Ugh. In the summer, when the sun had tanned my face and lightened my hair, I wasn't so bad. But in January, it was just dull, dull me. What if Fred's in love with me, I wondered. What if he wants to divorce Angie and marry me?

That night was the first time ever that I didn't finish my homework for English. I felt bad, but I couldn't keep my mind on dumb sentences like, "The boys had decided to surprise their mother by painting the fence while she was away." I had only finished three of the fifteen assigned sentences when I heard the Sloanes' van pull into their driveway. I put on my sweatshirt, gathered up my books, and met them at the front door.

"Everything okay?" Angie asked as she walked into the house.

"Fine," I said.

Angie went into the kitchen and got a glass of wine for herself and a can of beer for Fred.

"Do you want something before you go home, Cassie? It's early. How about a Coke or some ice cream?"

"I have to go," I said, my hand already on the doorknob.

"Fred, you'd better walk Cassie home," Angie said.

"No, it's okay," I told them. But Fred was right behind me, following me to the front door.

"Of course Fred will walk you, Cassie," Angie called after us. "He can pay on the way." She walked out to the end of the driveway with us. "What would your mother think if we let you walk home alone? Even Hamilton Heights has its share of crazies," she laughed. "Don't forget we need you Saturday night."

I kept my distance from Fred, feeling strange with him as we walked the two blocks to my house. He walked along, not looking at me or talking, looking at people's yards, looking up at the stars. It was a crisp, clear night.

As we turned into my driveway, Fred stopped and took some money from his back pocket. He walked on, counting out five one-dollar bills. Then he put the rest of the money back in his pocket and held the five ones out to me. When I reached to take them, he quickly grabbed my arm with his free hand and pulled me into the shadows at the side of our garage. He was so quick! He backed me against the garage and leaned his whole body hard against me.

"Stay here awhile," he whispered insistently. "No one will see us."

"I've got to go in. Please."

He leaned even harder against me. He pushed my head back with his hand, holding my chin tight. He put his mouth, open, over mine. It was sloppy wet and tasted of popcorn— salty and greasy and stale. I tried to squirm away but I was pinned flat against the wall.

"You're getting to be quite a babe, you know? These cute little bumps are getting bigger," he said, brushing his hand across my chest.

"I've got to go!" I pleaded.

Telling

He stood back a little. "Don't worry," he said. "You won't lose your cherry. We'll just have a little fun." He pressed the money into my hand and turned and walked back down the driveway and toward his house. I stood there, holding my money and watching him walk away. I wiped my face with the front of my sweatshirt. When I saw him turn the corner to his house, I got the key from under the flowerpot, opened the front door, put the key back in its place, and went into my house.

Usually my mom and dad are up around 11:00, but they were already in bed this night. I was glad. I didn't want to see anyone, or have anyone see me. I put my books on the desk, just inside my bedroom door. I pulled off my clothes and threw them in a heap on my closet floor. I went straight into the shower.

Sometimes my mother notices every little thing. It would have been just like her to want to know why I was taking a shower at night when I'd already had one in the morning and all that kind of stuff, so I was glad for my own bathroom connected to my bedroom, and that my parents' bedroom was down at the other end of the hall.

I made the water as hot as I could stand it and soaped my whole body twice. I bet I must have soaped my face eighty times. I even washed my hair. And after I brushed my teeth, I flossed. I always said I flossed, but I never did. But this night I actually flossed. I put on my favorite worn and washed thin flannel nightgown, the one my mother kept threatening to throw away. I looked at my English book one more time, but it was no use, so I climbed into bed and turned out the light.

I watched the patterns of the shadows on the wall opposite my window. There's a street light in front of our house, and even with my bedroom curtains closed, enough light comes in to cast shadows on the wall. Ever since I was small, I would lull myself to sleep by watching the changing patterns of light filtering through the eucalyptus tree and on through the curtains.

Sometimes the patterns seemed to be a shadowy dance, and I could hear music to go with it. Sometimes I would see children playing a game. When I was really little they played Ring-a-Round-a-Rosie and I guessed they were all at a birthday party, maybe my own. Later they played soccer, or Red Rover, Red Rover. At other times it was a big picnic scene, with lots of people and food. But this night the patterns wouldn't come together. Just when I would start to make something of them, they would shift—no dance, no games tonight.

I tried to say "The Lord's Prayer," but I could only say "Now I lay me down to sleep. I pray the Lord my soul to keep ... " I said that about fifteen times, but it didn't help. Fred Sloane's body, his popcorn breath, his insistent words, kept running through me.

I knew something was wrong. Fred's backing me against the wall was nothing like my Uncle Tom's backing me against a wall and making me plead for mercy. I knew it was something dirty because it felt dirty. I thought about rape. But it wasn't like what I'd heard about rape. I couldn't think about what happened with words. I just kept feeling it.

My mother had told me once that rape was when a man forced you to have sex with him. My cousin Lisa told me it was when a man pushed his thing in the private place between your legs and made you do it with him. She told me it was awful. I hadn't known exactly what my mother was talking about when she told me about rape. But I knew what Lisa meant.

I wished that Lisa was in my room with me that night, so I could tell her about Fred Sloane. Lisa's three years older than I am, but even when we were little she was real nice to me. She never tried to act like I was a baby, or like she knew everything and I didn't know anything, even though sometimes it seemed to me that she did know everything.

Lisa was the first one to tell me where babies really came from. Not that old story about when a mommy and daddy love each other they feel real close and daddy's sperm fertilizes mommy's egg and a little baby grows up in mommy's tummy until it's big enough to come out into the world. No, Lisa told me—I think I was about eight—babies get started when people have sex. And she told me exactly what "have sex" meant. She also told me the meaning of the "f" word.

Anyway, I always understood Lisa's explanations lots better than anyone else's, and I wondered what she could tell me about Fred. Maybe Mom would let me have Lisa over to spend the night tomorrow night. I could never have friends stay over on a weeknight. But Lisa could stay sometimes, because she was my cousin. Lisa and I didn't see each other so much, now that she was in high school. But we still had fun together like at Christmas and stuff.

Mom always liked it when Lisa and I got together. I think secretly she wanted me to be more like Lisa. I mean, Lisa's real cute, and she makes a good impression on adults.

It helped me to sleep, thinking about how maybe Lisa could come over and I could tell her what happened. Boy, did I want to see Lisa.

CHAPTER

C assie, get up. I'm making hot chocolate for Robbie. Want some?" I pulled the pillow over my head and turned my back to the doorway where Mom was standing.

"Cassie?"

"Okay, Mom, I heard. Thanks," I mumbled from under my pillow.

"Cassie!"

I pushed the pillow away and repeated my answer, this time so she could hear it. She turned and went down the hall. I thought about the night before, and Fred Sloane. Had he really kissed me like that? And talked to me that way? What did it mean?

I could hear Robbie in the kitchen. He loved to sing. He was singing "Pop, pop, fizz, fizz, oh what a relief it is," as he poured milk over his Rice Krispies. He sang in a monotone —a very loud monotone. He came up with some really weird combinations. Yesterday I'd heard him singing the alphabet song, "A, B, C, D, E, F, G, merrily down the stream."

I dragged myself out of bed and into the shower, thinking about how best to convince Mom that Lisa should spend the night.

Breakfast at our house is not exactly like at Wally and Beaver Cleaver's, with Ward and June all dressed up and everyone sitting together at the table. Mom's always running around half-dressed, trying to get Robbie to hurry up, and we don't even see Daddy in the mornings, except on weekends. He works at a bank in Century City, and he has to leave for work about 6:30 in the morning. There was already a cup of hot chocolate for me by the time I got to the table. There was some toast, too. I sat down across from Robbie, who was tearing his toast into little pieces and putting pieces into his cereal bowl.

Mom walked through, buttoning her blouse. "Get yourself some juice or fruit, Cassie."

"Juice or fruit, juice or fruit," Robbie chanted.

"Shut up, Robbie," I told him.

"Mom!" Robbie called.

"SHUT UP, ROBBIE," I hissed at him.

"Mommm," Robbie wailed. "Cassie keeps saying shut up to me."

Mom came sort of hopping back into the kitchen, wearing one leg of her special support panty hose and holding the other leg in her hand.

"Juice or fruit, Cassandra," she said, looking me straight in the eye for what seemed a long time. I didn't like those looks.

"Spank her, Mom. She keeps saying shut up to me."

"Robbie, can you remember the last time you saw me spank your sister?"

"No. But you better do it or she'll just keep on saying shut up, shut up, shut up, and you said you don't like people to say those words."

Robbie was really pleading his case, like he was a lawyer or something.

"Finish your breakfast, Robbie. We've got to leave in about five minutes," Mom said as she walked back to her bedroom. "Hurry up."

As soon as she left, I leaned over to Robbie and whispered, "Shut up!"

He took a breath to yell for Mom again, then thought better of it. He stuck his tongue out at me. I crossed my eyes at him. We started laughing. Robbie cracks me up when he laughs because once he gets started it's almost impossible for him to stop.

I carried my plate and cup to the dishwasher, poured myself about an inch of juice and carried it in with me to Mom's room. I wanted her to see me drinking it. She was almost ready to go. She was wearing a blue plaid skirt with a blue tailored blouse and a sort of maroon cardigan sweater. Her shoes were sensible—the kind older English teachers wear, even at Open House. She was a little bit older and a little bit fatter than most of my friend's mothers. I guess she looked okay, for her age. She was forty.

"I'm glad you got some juice, Cassie. I worry about your eating habits."

"Mom, could I ride with you and Robbie this morning? Could you drop me at Lisa's bus stop? It's near Robbie's school. It wouldn't be out of your way."

"You're not even ready yet, Cassie. I'm supposed to be at the daycare center by quarter to eight. Why do you want to do that anyway? You can't hang around Hamilton High with Lisa."

"I can get ready fast, Mom. And I can walk from Hamilton to Palm in about fifteen minutes. Okay?"

"Oh, okay. But if you're not ready by 7:35, we're leaving without you."

I rushed into my room, threw off my ratty old chenille robe and pulled a pair of jeans from my closet, thinking all the time about how I could talk Mom into letting Lisa spend the night. I was ready in about three minutes. My hair was still damp, but I could brush it dry in the car.

I opened the garage for Mom, put my books in the car and got into the front seat. Mom and Robbie came out a few minutes later. Robbie was carrying a Mickey Mouse lunchbox. He was wearing a Disneyland sweatshirt and a Mickey Mouse patch on the left knee of his blue jeans. When he first started kindergarten he used to always wear a Mickey Mouse hat with big mouse ears, but his teacher called Mom one day and said it was too distracting to the other kids, so Robbie couldn't wear his Mickey Mouse hat to school any more. He really did crack me up.

As soon as they got to the car, Robbie started in, "Why does she always get to sit in the front seat just because she's older? It's not fair." Mom just gave him one of her looks and he crawled back. We backed out of the garage and I got out and closed the door. When I got in again I asked, "Mom, could Lisa spend the night tonight? I need help with pre-algebra." I had my fingers crossed so she'd say yes, even though I don't really believe in that stuff.

"I thought you were doing well in math. Just last week you were telling me what a breeze it was."

"But we've started something new. It's harder now," I said. "And Lisa's real good at it. She can explain it real good." I was close to begging.

We turned the corner onto Primrose Avenue and nearly ran into Fred Sloane backing out of his driveway on his way to work at the muffler shop. As he stopped to let us pass, he honked the horn and waved. My stomach felt funny when I saw Fred. Robbie kept waving out the back window and yelling, "Hi, Fred, Hi, Fred," over and over again until we turned onto Main Street.

"Please, Mom. I need some help from Lisa." Seeing Fred Sloane made me feel like I had to talk to Lisa.

"Well … I guess it's all right. Just be sure you get that room of yours picked up and your bed made before she gets there. I'm embarrassed to have anyone see what a mess you live in."

"I'll clean it up. Thanks, Mom."

We pulled up in front of Robbie's school. He gave Mom a big slobbery kiss, yelled "bye" to me, and was out of the car almost the instant it stopped. We watched him walk up the steps to the kindergarten classroom, swinging his lunchbox, and then we drove the two blocks to Lisa's bus stop. Mom glanced over at me.

"Cassie, why are you wearing that jacket? Yesterday, when it was cold, you insisted on going out of the house in a short sleeve blouse with not even a sweater. Now today, when the sun is out like summertime, you're in that jacket zipped up to your neck! I swear, Cassie, sometimes I don't understand you at all," she said, shaking her head.

"Just let me out here, Mom. Lisa should be here any minute."

Telling

She stopped the car. As I was getting out, she took hold of my hand. I turned to her. She had this really serious look on her face.

"Cassie, Honey, I'm sorry. It seems like I'm nagging you a lot. I don't mean to. Let's do something fun, just the two of us, real soon."

"Sure, Mom. It's okay," I said. I was pretty sure we wouldn't do anything fun soon, but I couldn't think of much that was fun to do with my mom anyway. I got out of the car in a hurry, kind of embarrassed by her apology.

I walked down the street in the direction of Lisa's house. When I saw her, I was totally relieved that she was alone.

Lisa's popular, so she was usually with a lot of other kids. As soon as I saw her, I went running to meet her.

"Hey, C.C." (She calls me "C.C." because my name is Cassandra Camille.) "What are you doing down here?"

"Can you spend the night with me tonight, then we could watch a movie or something?"

"I don't even know if my mom would let me out on a Wednesday night."

"Oh, Lisa, she would, to our house. Please, Lisa." I just wanted to grab Lisa and beg her to say yes. I hadn't even considered that maybe Lisa couldn't, or wouldn't want to come over. All I had thought about was convincing my mom.

"I don't know, C.C. Diana said maybe she'd come home with me after school today. We're doing a debate in speech, and we've got to be ready by Friday."

I started to cry. I don't know why. I never cry except in the privacy of my own room, late at night, or in a really sad part of a movie, like in "E.T." We've got that videotape and Robbie loves it, and even though I've seen it a thousand times, I still cry at least once before it's over. But I think I really shocked Lisa by crying right there, in the morning, on the sidewalk, with no movie.

"C.C., C.C., C.C.," she kept saying, while I kept blubbering and wiping my nose on my jacket sleeve. Lisa looked up and down the street, like maybe she wanted to call for help, get the paramedics or something. When I saw how scared Lisa was, looking around frantically and repeating "C.C., C.C., C.C.," all of a sudden I saw how funny it was and I started laughing. I was laughing, but I was crying, too. Then Lisa started to laugh. We were laughing so hard we collapsed on the Coulter's lawn.

"Okay. Okay," Lisa gasped through her laughter. "I'll see if I can stay over."

We were still laughing, trying to catch our breath, when we saw the school bus turn the corner. We gathered up our books and went running, but I was so weak from laughing I dropped everything. Lisa had to run ahead and ask the driver to wait. I finally got on the bus and took a seat next to Lisa. Her friend Diana was sitting right in front of me. Diana casually took a compact from her purse, opened it, and held the mirror directly in front of my face. It's true. I looked pretty awful. My face was totally smeared from crying, and I had leaves in my hair. I felt really dumb. Diana had such a proper attitude.

After school that day I rushed home to clean my room, just like I had told Mom I would. I took off my jacket and stood in front of the mirror. What Fred had said was true. I was getting bigger. Almost all of the girls in my gym class wore bras. Mom had even bought me a pre-teen bra when school started this year. I tried it on after she brought it home. I hated it. It was stupid and uncomfortable. I liked undershirts. They were soft, and easy to put on. What did I care about any stupid old bra?

I stood in front of the mirror for a long time. Besides pooching out on top, my butt was getting bigger, too. I didn't think I liked what I saw. I put my jacket back on and zipped it up.

Robbie stays with Mom at the daycare center after he gets out of kindergarten. They'd only been home for a few minutes when Lisa came in. Sometimes I used to get disgusted with how Mom would be all slurpy over Lisa. This was one of those times.

4

"Lisa! How's my favorite niece?" Mom said, giving Lisa a big hug.

"Great, Auntie Helen," Lisa answered, smiling and showing both of the dimples in her cheeks. I know it's not Lisa's fault she has dimples, but there are times when I wish she weren't so cute.

"I just love that skirt, Auntie Helen. Can I help with dinner?" Boy, did Lisa ever know how to kiss up to my mom.

"No, Honey. You and Cassie go on and get to work on Cassie's math. I think she needs plenty of help."

Lisa gave me a funny look, but she didn't say anything. "Come on, Lisa," I said, already on my way down the hall.

We went to my room and closed the door.

"Math?" Lisa asked, raising her eyebrows.

"Well … I didn't really want to talk to you on the phone. I didn't want anyone to hear me."

Just then Robbie came bursting into my room, carrying a deck of cards.

"I can play Fish, Lisa. Let's play Fish."

"Okay, Robbie. You deal," Lisa said.

That's something else that sometimes disgusts me with Lisa. She's too patient with Robbie. I guess if she'd had a little brother she wouldn't have been so patient. Lisa was an only child though, so she thought having a little brother was some kind of big deal. I watched her as she sat cross-legged on the bed, gathering up her cards. Her hair was thick and shiny black. Her eyes were dark, dark brown, and her skin was creamy white. There was nothing dull about her. Everything seemed to shine. Next to her, Robbie looked kind of dull, like me.

Robbie dealt the cards again, half of them face up. He and Lisa proceeded to play a second hand of Fish. Lisa let Robbie win. It was easy to let Robbie win if you wanted to because he was such a cheat.

No sooner was the game finished than it was dinner time. Another thing that burned me was that whenever Lisa was at our house Mom would fix Lisa's favorite chicken enchilada casserole. I just happened to hate chicken enchilada casserole. When I visited Lisa's house we were lucky if Aunt Trudy fixed anything, much less my favorite. I bet she didn't even know if I had a favorite food or not. I liked Aunt Trudy though. She always had funny stories to tell about her work at the Children's Hospital. You wouldn't think she'd see a lot of funny stuff there, but she did.

Anyway, by the time Lisa had oohhed and aahhed over the meal, and Daddy had quizzed her about her vocational banking class, and Robbie had been sent from the table for talking with his mouth full for the millionth time, and Mom had complained because I didn't appreciate the chicken casserole when millions of children were starving all over the world, and all of that, I began to think I would never even get to talk with Lisa in private. Luckily, though, it was Daddy and Robbie's turn to do the dishes, so Lisa and I were free to talk right after dinner. We went back to my room again. I didn't really know how to start. We were quiet for a while, kind of like we didn't know each other very well any more. Finally I said, "Lisa, has a man ever kissed you? Not a relative, but just some man?"

"Raymond," she said. "I thought he never would and then finally last Saturday night, standing on the porch, he did it. He kissed me. He's so shy, I thought I would have to kiss him first."

"No, not like a boyfriend, or someone your own age. I mean like a man, maybe old enough to be your dad, or your uncle."

"Well … " She paused, thinking. "Old Mr. Reed, when he gave me pennies, always used to ask me to kiss him. That was long ago. He never kissed me. He just … "

Lisa stopped talking and looked at me. "What are you getting at, C.C.? Why are you asking me about men and kissing?"

"Something weird happened last night."

"What was it?" she asked.

"I don't know how to tell you," I said.

"Just tell me, C.C.! You got me over here so you could tell me something. So now tell me!"

So I told her about how Fred Sloane had grabbed me and held me and pushed his tongue into my mouth. And I told her what he'd said about me getting to be a babe. I know it sounds funny, but I felt kind of important and grown-up. I mean, Lisa had always been the one to tell me stuff about boys and sex and here she was, looking totally shocked and attentive. When I finished she just sat there.

"Fred Sloane?" she said. "Fred Sloane?" she repeated, her voice high pitched. "That slime! Somebody ought to go kick him where it hurts! Somebody ought to call the cops on that slime!" Her voice was getting louder and louder.

"Shhh, Lisa, someone might hear you!"

"So what if they do?" she said. "Someone should hear me! That slime!"

I was pretty scared. "Please, Lisa," I said, and I started to cry again. I couldn't believe it. Years without crying in public, except for movies, and today I'd already cried twice in front of Lisa. I didn't want to cry, but I couldn't stop myself. Anyway, when I started crying Lisa calmed down.

"What are you going to do, C.C.? What if he rapes you? Aren't you scared?"

"I don't know. I just feel funny about it. What if maybe he loves me?"

"Loves?" She gave me a strange look. "Did you like what he did? Did it seem like he loved you?"

"Well, no. I didn't like it. He was so … pushy. And I didn't like him talking about my bumps, or my cherry. What does cherry mean, anyway, Lisa?"

"C.C.! I can't believe you. Your cherry is your hymen. You know, the little thing like tough skin I guess, that's supposedly not broken until you have sex, like, all the way, except I think sometimes it gets broken if you fall, or ride your bicycle wrong, or something."

"Did he mean he wouldn't go all the way with me when he said that?"

"I guess so. But how could you believe a slime like that?"

"He's not really a slime, Lisa. I mean, he's always been nice to me before."

"C.C.!" Her voice was getting shrill again. "He's a pervert!"

I started to cry again. "I don't know what to do. What if Angie finds out? I like Angie. She's like one of my best friends, even if she is older. Maybe I can just not be around Fred when I go over there."

"Will you go over there again?"

"Well, I'm supposed to babysit Saturday night. They're going to this party and Angie asked me a long time ago to save Saturday night. I told her I would, but now I don't know what to do."

"You should tell your mom and dad."

"No! I almost couldn't tell you, and I always think I can tell you anything."

"I'd tell my mom."

"Yeah, but your mom's a lot different than my mom."

"Well … What will you do?"

"I don't know. It's like I'll never feel the same, you know?"

"How?"

"I'll never feel the same about Fred Sloane again. Like I don't really know him anymore … Has anything like that ever happened to you, Lisa?"

"No! I don't know what I'd do, either … Karen, she's in my gym class, and we were both on the bench one day because we were excused, and she told me her uncle tried stuff with her."

"What did she do?"

"She said she'd always hide when he came over to their house. It's strange. She said he was her favorite uncle until a year or so ago, and then he started that stuff. You know, putting his hands all over her and everything."

We talked a long time that night, and then we started in on our homework. Lisa curled up with her books on one bed, and I curled up on the other. When I was ten, Robbie got my old youth bed, and I got to choose new beds and curtains and everything for my room. I think I did a pretty good job, for only being ten. The walls were white. The curtains and bedspreads were red with white checks, and there was a red rug on the floor. I had lots of pictures of animals on the walls. I like animals a lot, but my mom will never let us have pets.

Anyway, that night we'd work for a while and talk for a while. I made up the English homework I'd missed from the night before and answered the questions from my geography book. Lisa told me more about Raymond. She told me about her banking instructor, and how hard Hamilton High was in comparison to Palm Avenue Junior High School. She told me about how some of her friends smoked pot at a party a week ago, and how stupid they acted.

I told her about Jason, who kept dropping notes into my locker, and how Mr. Stanley had a heart attack right in the middle of math, and the ambulance came and took him to the hospital. But we always came back to Fred Sloane.

Lisa said, "I used to think he was kind of good looking, but I'll never look at him again without thinking Slimy Sloane." We laughed about that, but I felt kind of guilty—disloyal, or something. He had been real nice to me sometimes.

Having Lisa there that night helped a lot. I didn't feel so numb after that, and I could think about other things besides just what Fred had done to me. In the morning though, Lisa and I went with Mom to Lisa's bus stop. Just as we were getting out, Mom said, "Cassie, I almost forgot to tell you. Angie called while you were in the shower this morning. She said she was expecting you to babysit Saturday night. I told her you'd be there. Have a good day at school, girls." And then she drove off.

I looked at Lisa, helplessly. Lisa said, "Don't worry, we'll figure something out. Call me tonight. I'll put my computer-like brain to work on this."

Just then the bus came along. We both got on, and Lisa was lost to me in her crowd of friends, including snotty Diana. I almost started crying, but I held it back.

CHAPTER

5

I ran all the way from Hamilton High to Palm that morning. I carried my books and lunch in a nylon backpack. It bounced against my back with every step I took. I could smell the banana in my lunch sack turning to mush.

Mandy yelled at me as I went running past the first gate.

"Cassie! Help! Cassie! I need your geography homework."

Mandy almost always needed my geography homework. It used to make me mad sometimes. She'd copy my geography answers while she sat in the back of our first period English class. She'd get the same little homework checks in Garcia's pukey green roll book as I would. Then she'd come in with these ninety-eight point test scores and end up with an A on her report card. I'd get a B and a comment from my parents that I could be doing A work if I tried harder.

Still, Mandy was my best friend. We'd been Bluebirds together when almost everyone else was in Brownies. That kind of experience cements friendships I guess. I handed her my homework.

"Thanks, Cassie. You're a pal, a buddy, a true friend."

I didn't have an answer. I was thinking about how I would tell my mother off for the way she set me up for babysitting.

She was always doing stuff like that, telling people I'd do something when she didn't even know if I wanted to or not. It made me angry.

"Cassie? Are you mad at me, your old pal, your old buddy, your true friend?" Mandy was looking at me with this simple, pleading grin. She had the bluest eyes I'd ever seen on anyone, and she could get this absolutely innocent look on her face. She had corn-silk blonde hair and light freckles. The way she was looking at me right then reminded me of how she used to look in kindergarten. That's how long we've been friends. I smiled.

"No, I'm not mad at you. I'm kind of mad at my mom."

"Why? Is she threatening to turn your room into a thrift shop again?"

"Ha-ha. You're soooo funny," I said, in my most sarcastic way.

"Really. Why are you mad at your mom?"

"Oh, she promised Angie Sloane I'd babysit there Saturday night and she didn't even ask me if I wanted to or not. She always thinks she can just decide things for me without even asking. I wish she'd butt out!"

Mandy rolled her eyes heavenward. "Your mother! Francine's always making plans for me to wash windows for everyone in the whole neighborhood. She says it's good, clean work."

Mandy's a trip. She started calling her mother "Francine" in the sixth grade. She told me she thought "Mother" and "Mom" distorted their relationship.

"I don't know what to do about babysitting. I guess I'm stuck with it," I said.

We took our seats in the back of the room. I was supposed to sit second from the front row, next to the windows, but I traded with Valerie Biggers the first week of school. Old Marlow spent about ten minutes each morning taking roll from his seating chart, checking and double checking and filling out the little white slips for the attendance office, but he never caught on about the seat trade. Whenever Valerie was absent, I sat in my assigned seat, and vice versa, but we both hardly ever missed school, so that was no problem.

Marlow was wearing his first-week-of-the-month sport

coat with his Wednesday-through-Friday blue K-Mart shirt and his first-week-of-the-month brown polyester pants. I'd never have noticed his clothing patterns, except that he always looked rumpled. But Mandy kept a little chart on the first page of her notebook where she marked down each day what each of her teachers wore. She said you could tell a lot about a person that way, and the more you knew about a teacher, the better the grade you got. She always got good grades, but I think it was because she was smart, like getting ninety-eight points on geography tests when she hardly ever looked at the book.

Marlow seemed pretty dense about some things, like taking roll, and getting names straight, and just getting his shirt buttoned right. But he was okay once he got going. Thursday was writing day and he told us, "Write about a time when you've been angry with one of your parents. Just write in any form. Whatever comes to you, write it down."

Mandy leaned over and whispered, "He must have read your mind."

I had already started writing. I started with how it made me angry when my mom made plans for me without even talking to me about it. I wrote about how she'd never let us have pets, and how Robbie could do whatever he wanted and not get into trouble, but I couldn't do the least little thing without having Mom jump all over me. I was just getting warmed up when Marlow said, "Okay. Put it in correct form. Remember topic sentences, supporting details, examples, and please remember I can't stand to be bored. If yours is the paper I fall asleep over, it's an automatic 'F'."

After English, Mandy and I had gym together. We were on the seventh grade girls' soccer team, so we always got to practice soccer second period. The rest of the class did dumb exercises and stupid modern dance stuff, like pretending you're some tree waving in the breeze.

When I got home from school I tried to talk to my mom about saying yes for me without asking.

"But Angie told me she'd already asked you to save

Saturday night. And I knew you didn't have any plans."

"Sometimes I just don't want to babysit," I told Mom. "I don't always have to babysit, do I? It's a free country, isn't it?"

"Well, I'm sorry, Miss Democracy. I'll have to be more careful next time," she said, pulling herself up about two inches in height and looking down at me. My mom always got bigger when she got mad. Dad came into the kitchen where we were talking.

"What's going on?" he asked, opening the refrigerator door and peering inside. "How come we never have anything to snack on around here?"

"Maybe because you never go to the market!" Mom yelled. She stomped out of the kitchen and into the bedroom, slamming the door behind her.

"Oops, wrong thing to say," Dad said, smiling at me.

"Well, we don't ever have anything to snack on around here," I agreed.

"Is that your mother's fault?" Dad asked. I hated it when he asked those kinds of questions. I knew it was a trap, and pretty soon he'd be telling me I should help with the grocery shopping, even if he was the one who had started complaining in the first place. I went into the den and called Lisa.

"Did you get out of babysitting at Slimy Sloane's?"

"No. I can't get out of it."

"C.C.! Just tell them what happened!" Lisa said in her most exasperated voice.

"Be serious, Lisa. I can't do that. Besides, I'm mad at them both. I don't want to talk to them for a month."

"But C.C., this is important. What will you do?"

"I'll just babysit. It's no big deal."

"It is too a big deal."

She was right, I knew, but I just couldn't figure out what else to do. "Maybe you could come with me?" I said.

"I would, but Raymond's got the car Saturday night. We're even going out to dinner."

There was a long silence on the phone, then I suggested, "Maybe I could run away. Like just for a week or something."

"Don't be stupid, C.C. Where would you go?"

"I could hide in the garage."

"C.C. … " Lisa was beginning to sound disgusted with me. "I know what we can do. I'll have Raymond drop me off at the Sloanes' Saturday night. His dad will only let him keep the car out until 11:00 anyway. So I'll come to the Sloanes. They won't be home until late, will they? And then you and I can walk back to your house together."

"Could you, Lisa? That's great!"

"C.C.? Just remember not to let him get you alone when you get there. Just hang around Angie until they leave. Okay?"

"Yeah, I will. No way will Fred catch me alone in the living room this time."

I was so relieved when I hung up from talking with Lisa, I almost forgot to be mad at Mom. When I went back into the kitchen, Mom and Daddy had their arms around each other and were laughing. I heard Mom say, "Death to male chauvinist pigs," and then she started poking Daddy in the ribs. I couldn't hear what Daddy was saying because he was laughing so hard. I wasn't mad anymore.

Usually when I babysat at the Sloanes' I went a little early so I could talk with Angie. Saturday night, I waited until the last minute and arrived exactly at 7:30. They were ready to go when I got there. Fred opened the door for me and I walked in and stood right next to Angie. Even when she went back to their room to get her coat, I followed her.

"Do you want me to hang up your jacket for you, Cassie?" she asked. I guess she thought that was why I was standing in front of her closet.

"Oh, no. I'll just wear it for a while."

"Don't you think it's kind of warm in here for a jacket?"

Tina and Dorian came running in before I had to answer Angie. Dorian had a new Pop-Up book and he wanted me to read it to him right then.

"Wait, Dorian," Angie said. "Cassie can read to you when we're gone."

"Angie, is it okay for my cousin Lisa to come over after awhile? She's going to walk home with me and spend the night at my house."

"Sure, Cassie. Help yourself to food if you want anything. We should be back around 1:00."

Fred came back to the bedroom. "Let's go, Angie. What're you two yapping about anyway?"

It was like he was kidding, but he looked kind of mad.

"I'm ready, Honey. Just last minute touches. How do I look?" She flashed him a smile, striking a modeling pose.

"You look great," he said, and he sounded like he really meant it.

Angie really did look great, too. It must have been some fancy party, because they were both totally dressed up. Angie was wearing a blue dress with tiny shoulder straps. The dress was made of some kind of light, slinky material. Fred was in a suit. I'd never seen him in a suit before. It was blue, too, but it was navy blue. He was wearing a vest, and a light blue shirt with a red and blue striped tie. Just looking at Fred, and trying not to think about the other stuff, I thought, truthfully, he looked pretty great, too.

I walked out of the room and down the hall just in front of Angie, with Fred walking behind. Dorian and Tina kissed them both good night, and they left, just like that. I did the usual with the two kids, and then watched TV for a while. Lisa got to the Sloanes' about 10:30. We watched some old Cary Grant, Grace Kelly movie, and Lisa talked on and on about Raymond and dinner at the Spaghetti Factory.

The Sloanes got back about 12:30, Angie paid me, Lisa and I said good night, and that was it. I would almost have thought I'd imagined the whole thing with Fred Sloane, except that as we walked out the front door, we walked past him. He was standing there holding the door open for us. Lisa was right in front of me, and Angie was standing in the hallway. As I walked out the door he stepped behind me and slipped his hand up between my legs!

"Thanks, Cassie," he said, pulling his hand away with a squeeze.

"'Night, Cassie and Lisa," Angie called from the hallway.

On the way down the driveway Lisa said to me, "I guess we took care of Slimy Sloane tonight, didn't we? He did look kind of handsome though, huh, Cassie?"

Telling

When I told her what he'd done at the door, she just stopped and stared at me.

"But Angie was standing right behind him. How could he?"

"I guess the way he was standing, maybe Angie couldn't see his hands."

"I can't believe he'd do that," Lisa told me. "They look like the perfect couple."

"I know. But he did it for sure," I said.

"If I heard that from anyone but you, C.C., I don't know if I'd believe them."

"Yeah. I almost don't believe it myself. He always seems so nice."

"He must have had a lot of practice to be able to get away with that stuff right in front of Angie," Lisa said. "What do you think would have happened if I hadn't been there and he'd have taken you home?"

"I don't know, Lisa. I'm really glad you came over tonight."

When we got back to my house and climbed into bed, we whispered until it was almost time for the sun to come up. Lisa still thought I should tell my parents and I still didn't want to. It was strange. Lisa seemed to be more scared than I was. I guess I still couldn't get past the feeling that Fred was my friend. I really didn't think he would hurt me.

Lisa talked for a while about Raymond—how nice he was and how she wanted him to keep asking her out. I wondered what it would be like to have a boyfriend. Mandy thought Jason liked me, because of the notes in my locker and all, but Jason wasn't really a boyfriend to me like Raymond was to Lisa. Usually Jason's notes were just cartoons he'd cut from the newspaper with arrows drawn to funny looking characters and my name at the end of the arrows.

I think I fell asleep first.

It seemed like I'd only been asleep about ten minutes when I heard Aunt Trudy's gruff voice.

"Wake up. Wake up. Don't waste your day asleep in the

hay," she yelled as she moved to open my curtains and let the sun in. She sat down on Lisa's bed and started bouncing up and down.

It's hard to believe Aunt Trudy and my mom are sisters. Lisa and I used to pretend that one of them was adopted, but Grammy convinced us that they were both her natural born children. My mom is about 5'3" and a little on the chubby side. Her hair is like mine, kind of mousy brown. She wears sensible clothing, usually skirts and blouses. Even when she gets dressed up she looks sensible.

Aunt Trudy is about 5'8" and she's so skinny her bones stick out. And she always wears a lot of eye makeup. This morning she was wearing her bright orange dashiki tied at the waist with a purple, woven belt. Her earrings were long purple feathers and her eye shadow matched her earrings. Her lipstick matched her dashiki. In a way, I guess you could say she was color coordinated. Oh, yes. Her hair. Her hair was a strawberry blonde with dark roots, and it just kind of stuck out all over her head. Daddy said Aunt Trudy's style was a cross between Phyllis Diller and Punk.

Lisa was already out in the kitchen by the time I dragged out of bed. Aunt Trudy had brought bagels, lots of them, and everyone was sitting around the table munching away. I like Sunday mornings like that.

I'd just started on my second cinnamon bagel when the phone rang. It was Angie, wanting to know if I could babysit again next Saturday night.

"I'm not sure yet," I said. "Can I call you back later?"

When I hung up, Mom said, "You're not doing anything Saturday night, are you? You could use the money."

I didn't answer. Lisa and I just looked at each other. I didn't finish my bagel.

6

It was really stupid of me, but I kept babysitting at the Sloanes. It was hard coming up with believable excuses not to babysit. I mean, how busy can a twelve-year-old tomboy's calendar be? And it wasn't just making excuses to Angie. Mom always had to be convinced, too.

I was careful. Like, I usually babysat on Fred's bowling night. Angie would often go out with friends when Fred went bowling. On those nights he left before Angie did, and she always got home first. Or if I knew Lisa could come with me, then I'd babysit. Even being so careful though, Fred managed some sneak moves. I was pretty sure he'd do more if he got the chance.

I kept looking forward to summer. Except for last year, when she was in Europe, Robbie and I always stayed with our grandmother during the summer. She lived in a mobile home over in Santa Monica, not far from the beach. I held on to June in my mind, like all of my problems would just go away for the summer.

In May, on one of those safe bowling nights, Fred came home early. As soon as I heard his motorcycle turn the corner, I walked out the front door. I knew it was safer to meet him in front, even when it was nighttime, than it was to wait for him in the house. Just as I got out the door though, Tina let out a scream. I ran to her bedroom.

"Tina, what is it?"

"Big monster, big monster," she sobbed.

"It was a bad dream," I said, picking her up and holding her. She was still sobbing when Fred came into the room.

"What's the trouble, Pumpkin?" he asked, taking her from my arms and smoothing her hair.

"A monster," she told him, "but it's gone now, Daddy."

Fred gently put her back in bed and pulled the covers around her. I had been so involved with Tina, I had forgotten to be careful of Fred. I quickly walked out of the room and down the hall toward the door.

Fred caught me at the end of the hall. He put his arms around my waist and pulled me to him, my back against his body. It was not rough though, just firm. He whispered to me, his cheek rubbing against the top of my head.

"You're a tough kid to catch alone. You know I won't hurt you."

I felt his lips on the back of my neck, his warm breath and then the wetness of his tongue just under my ear. His hands moved gently, firmly, from my waist down to my abdomen, down my thighs and then back up along the inside of my thighs, stopping between my legs, gripping tightly. I didn't fight. I didn't move. Something kept me there. He kept one hand between my legs while he turned me to him with the other. He put his face to mine, lips to mine, his tongue moving first along the edge of my lips and then into my mouth. He moved both hands to my butt and began pushing, rubbing his body against mine. He groped for the buttons on my jeans, trying to undo them. I pushed at him, and began to fight.

"No, Baby. No. Please. I need this." All the time pushing, rubbing.

"Let me go," I gasped.

"Oh, Honey," he breathed at me. "I'll be good to you. You're gonna love this. Please, Baby."

He was breathing fast. His eyes were half closed and he was pushing harder. I got scared. Really scared.

"Let me go! Let me go!" I began to cry and yell at the same time. His pleading mood changed instantly.

"Shut up!" he hissed, pushing harder still. Then I heard

Angie's car pull into the driveway. Fred let go and went down the hall to the bathroom. I ran out the front door and down the driveway. Angie was just getting out of the car.

"Wait, Cassie, I brought us some ice cream."

"I can't," I yelled back, running to the street. I heard her call my name once more, but I kept running as fast as I could 'til I got to my house. The front door was unlocked. I burst in, still running, to my bedroom, slamming first the front door and then my bedroom door behind me. I threw myself across my bed and just lay there, panting. My parents were already in bed watching the eleven o'clock news.

"Cassie! Lock the door," Mom yelled down the hall.

"Lock it yourself!" I yelled back.

"Cassie!"

I got up and locked the front door, went back to my room, slamming my bedroom door again, this time harder. I filled my bathtub full of steaming hot water and some old Snoopy bubble bath stuff. I put my clothes in the hamper in my bathroom and climbed into the tub. I was still scared. I was afraid to think about what might have happened if Angie hadn't come when she did. I slid down the tub so that my whole body was submerged. I put the steaming hot washcloth over my face. I relived the whole scene with Fred Sloane. Partly, mostly, I was repulsed by it. I couldn't get clean enough, my body, my mouth. I kept using more soap and adding more hot water. I even washed my mouth out with soap. Partly too, though, a little, I wanted to think about what might have happened if Angie hadn't come home when she did. In bed that night I curled up into a little tiny ball, the way Daddy said I always used to sleep when I was a baby. "You were a cocoon kid," he would laugh. That night I tried to be a cocoon kid again. My knees were drawn up, touching my forehead, my hands folded between my legs, where Fred Sloane's hands had been.

I dreamt I was in a huge, two-story house with no windows. I was in an empty room, both doors locked, but there was a trap door in the floor which I could open. From the trap door there was a very long ladder leading down to a basement, a furnace room. The furnace was roaring with fire, and the heat was unbearable. It looked as if the only way out was to run past the furnace and up the steps on the other side. I had to get out. I awoke, sweaty and sticky and crying.

First thing in the morning, before I was even out of bed, I heard Angie and Mom talking at the front door.

"Cassie left in such a hurry last night—I didn't even get a chance to pay her."

"Thanks, Angie. I'll give it to her. She was in one of her little snits last night."

"I guess kids usually save that sort of thing for their parents, huh, Helen? She always seems like the model girl in our house."

"Oh, Angie. Just wait until Tina and Dorian hit adolescence! You just don't know," Mom said with a laugh.

I hated it when she talked about me that way, like I was some kind of adolescent idiot or something and she was the know-it-all mother.

"Well, if Tina and Dorian are as nice as Cassie, I won't worry," I heard Angie tell Mom. "Fred says he never worries about the kids when Cassie's with them. She's so level headed …"

I went into the shower so I wouldn't have to hear any more of their stupid babbling. They didn't know me at all!

I was all ready for school by the time Mom and Robbie left. Mom asked if I wanted a ride, but I said I'd rather walk. I started out for school and then did something I'd never done before. I turned around and came back home. I cut school. I hadn't even planned it. I just turned around without thinking.

I was a little numb again. Like I had been after the first time Fred Sloane grabbed me and kissed me and talked about my cherry. I watched the rest of the "Today Show." I wondered what Katie Couric would have done if she were in my place. I couldn't figure it out. I watched a rerun of "I Love Lucy," and then I called Grammy Healy.

"Cassie? What a nice surprise. How are you, Honey?"

"Fine, Grammy. Am I still coming to stay with you when school's out?"

Telling

"Well, I hope so! There's a new pizza place just down the street from me. You can swim every day, and then we'll eat pizza and go to the movies every night. Don't tell your mother, though," Grammy laughed.

"Grammy? Could I please come stay some weekend before summer?"

"Oh, Cassie, that would be wonderful. Tell your folks to bring you anytime. Just call me a day or so ahead of time and I'll sweep all those old codgers off my doorstep."

"Okay. Thanks."

"Cassie? Why aren't you in school today?"

I thought fast. "Teacher work day," I answered. It wasn't exactly a lie. I supposed teachers were working even if I wasn't there. "Bye, Grammy. I'll see you real soon."

I felt a little better after I talked with Grammy. I got some ice cream from the freezer. There was only a little in the carton, so I poured some chocolate syrup in, and some raisin-granola, and went back to the TV. I started watching "The Flintstones," but they were too stupid even for me. I switched to "Days of Our Lives." Someone was falling in love with someone else's husband. I turned off the TV and went into my parents' bedroom. They have a big king-sized bed, with lots of pillows and a down comforter. When I was real little, if I was sick, Mom would let me sleep in there and bring me juice and stuff and read to me. I crawled into their bed and went to sleep. I was still in their bed, watching Oprah talk to husbands of abusive women, when Mom and Robbie got home.

"What are you doing in here?" Mom asked.

"I just felt like watching TV here," I said.

Robbie came running in and threw himself on the bed as Mom walked out to the kitchen. He began poking and tickling me and rolling all over the bed. As I started to get up, he threw his arms around me and started kissing me. He put his lips on mine and stuck his tongue in my mouth.

"Robbie!" I pushed him back, shocked. "Why did you do that? What's the matter with you, anyway? Why did you do that with your tongue?"

Robbie looked scared.

"What's wrong with that, anyway? Dorian does that. Tina does that. That's how their dad kisses."

"Oh, Robbie," was all I could say.

"So! You're not my mom!" Robbie yelled as he stomped out of the room. When Mom came in to get me to help, I told her I was really sick and I wanted to be left alone.

"Then get into your own room, Cassie. Keep your germs to yourself."

Daddy came in to talk with me when he got home from work.

"What's wrong, Cassie?" he asked. He looked so worried that I almost wanted to tell him, but I was afraid. I didn't know how to start.

"I think I'm getting the flu," I said.

"Well, just stay here and rest, Sweetheart. Call us if you need anything."

I knew he meant it, to call him if I needed anything. I just didn't know how to do that. I felt awful.

Mom came in after dinner and sat on my bed. "I'm going to a meeting at the daycare center tonight, Cassie, but Dad and Robbie will be here."

I pretended to be asleep. I didn't want to talk to anyone, least of all Mom. She shook my shoulder. "Cassie?" I still pretended to be asleep.

"Cassie? Come on, wake up for a minute."

I groaned and pushed the pillow away from my face. "What? Can't you just leave me alone?"

"I need to talk with you for a minute, and I'm leaving now," Mom said. She sounded irritated with me, but I didn't care.

"I didn't wake you earlier because I thought you needed your rest, but Lisa called. She wants you to call her back."

"Tomorrow," I said, pulling the pillow back over my head.

"She said it was important, something about you helping her with a math assignment for a change." Mom laughed. "Lisa must really be desperate for help."

I kept the pillow over my head.

Telling

"I think you should call her, Cassie. She always helps you."

"Leave me alone!" I shouted, and buried myself further under the covers and pillow.

I felt her looking at me. I knew she was angry. But then she got up from my bed and left, closing the door behind her. Why couldn't people just leave me alone? I wanted to stay huddled under all of my covers, with my pillow over my head. Maybe I would never want to come out. What did Lisa want? It must have been something to do with the Fred Sloane thing or why would she talk about help with a math assignment?

About an hour after Mom left, I heard the muffled ring of our telephone, then Daddy came to my door and opened it a crack.

"Cassie, it's Lisa," he said softly. I didn't respond. "She says it's important. Why don't you come talk to her?"

"I just don't feel like it," I told him. "I'll call her first thing in the morning."

He closed the door again. I stayed burrowed under the covers. I wished I had about ten more blankets on my bed. I wanted to feel buried. Later, but before Mom came home, I thought I heard Aunt Trudy's voice, but then I thought maybe it was a dream. It wasn't a dream, though. The voices got louder. I started to pay attention. Just as I pulled my head out from under the pillow so I could hear better, Daddy flung open my bedroom door, turned on the light, and demanded, "Get up, Cassie! Right now!"

7

My heart sank when I saw Aunt Trudy, Uncle Tom, and Lisa sitting together on the couch in our living room. I sat on the footstool across from them. Lisa's eyes were all red. She came over and sat beside me.

"I had to tell, C.C. I was scared."

"Tell what?" I asked. Boy, can I come up with some stupid questions.

Daddy was sitting on the edge of his chair, leaning forward. His face was practically right in front of mine.

"Why in the hell didn't you tell us about this Fred Sloane business, Cassie?"

"You could have been raped. Both of you. You never know how a person like that will behave!" Aunt Trudy said.

While she was talking I was whispering to Lisa, "Why did you tell? You promised you wouldn't."

"How long has this been going on?" Daddy asked. Uncle Tom, who had been sitting with his arms folded, staring at the ceiling, stood up.

"Les, Trudy, we can't all talk at once. This is getting us nowhere," he said. "Let's hear what Cassie has to say." Lisa was explaining to me why she told our secret, but she stopped after her dad spoke.

"Please, I want to hear what Lisa's telling me first," I said.

Lisa started over again, and everyone listened.

"I was walking home from Diana's after school today, and I walked past the muffler shop where Fred works. He saw me and came walking out to the sidewalk. He caught up with me and told me to tell my hot-pants cousin he knows what she wants. And he smiled this really sick smile. He started to say something else, but his boss, Mr. Casteneda, called him back. I don't know why it scared me so much, but it did. Something about him just made me feel creepy."

Aunt Trudy said, "I could tell as soon as I saw her something was wrong. Remember how she looked when she was learning to swim—her little face all tight and fearful? That was the look she had when she came in this afternoon. When I heard what had been going on, I wanted to come over right away. Lisa insisted on talking to Cassie first, but when she wouldn't come to the phone after the fifth try, we came ahead."

"I'm really sorry, C.C. Are you mad at me?"

I shook my head. "I guess not, it's just that you promised."

"Damn it, Cassie!" Daddy shouted. "She did exactly the right thing. She did exactly what you should have done in the very beginning!"

I started to cry. Daddy never swears. It was a shock to hear him talk that way.

"Who are you mad at, Les?" Uncle Tom said in his slow, deliberate way. Then he looked at me for a minute. I was crying. Everyone was quiet.

Daddy looked at me. "I'm sorry, Cassie, if it sounds like I'm mad at you. I'm not. Tell us what happened."

My throat closed up. I couldn't think of what to say.

"Tell them how he kissed you, and how he talked to you, C.C.," Lisa urged.

So I did. I told them about that first night when Fred pushed me against the wall and kissed me, and all that he'd said. I told them how Lisa and I had worked things out and how I'd thought everything would be okay when I went to Grammy's in June.

"When's the last time Sloane tried anything with you?" Uncle Tom asked.

"Last night," I answered. I told them how Fred had come

home early, and how I'd been more scared than I'd ever been before. I told them about how Robbie had kissed me with his tongue, and how he'd said that Tina and Dorian and Fred all kissed like that so it was okay.

Aunt Trudy groaned. "He really must be some kind of pervert. Do you think we should call the police?"

There was a long silence. "I don't know what to do," Daddy said. "What I want to do is go over there and beat him senseless! I know that's not really an answer, though."

Uncle Tom looked at his watch. "It's eleven o'clock," he announced. "We're not going to make any decisions tonight anyway, especially without Helen. Let's get some sleep." He stood up to leave. We all got up. Uncle Tom came over to me and Lisa and put his arms around us both. Then Daddy and Aunt Trudy did the same thing. The five of us stood in a big hug for a minute, and then they left.

I started to go back to my bedroom.

"We have to wait up for your mother, Cassie," Daddy said. "She has to hear this, too."

"I don't want to tell her," I said.

"But you must. We're all in this together now, and she's got to know."

"Can't you just tell her?" I asked.

"No. You've got to do it. But I'll help," he said. Just as he said that, Mom opened the back door.

"What a meeting! Some people are unbelievably crazy."

"Yeah, well wait until you hear this," Daddy said, and began to tell the Fred Sloane story.

"He's been after Cassie, kissing her, putting his hands all over her, all but raping her ... " I could feel him getting mad all over again.

"Fred Sloane?" Mom said, staring at me. "Fred Sloane?" Her voice went up so high it didn't even sound like her.

"Yes. Fred Sloane. When Cassie goes to babysit he takes every possible opportunity to get his filthy hands on her. Fred Sloane." Daddy was practically yelling.

"Why didn't you tell us, Cassie? What's the matter with

you? Where was Angie when all this was going on?" Mom was asking questions so fast I couldn't answer any of them. "Well, Cassie? Answer me. Why didn't you tell us?"

"I dunno," was all I could mumble.

"She was embarrassed," Daddy said, "and scared. She turned to Lisa for help. That's how I found out, just now. Trudy and Tom and Lisa just left a few minutes ago."

Mom just sat there, looking at me. "Exactly what did Mr. Sloane do to you, Cassie?"

"He kissed me. And he touched me," I mumbled.

"Speak up, Cassie. I can't even hear you," Mom said harshly.

"Just what Dad told you," I answered, starting to cry again. I didn't want to talk about it anymore. I wanted summer to be here and to go to Grammy's and never, ever think about Fred Sloane again. I went into the bathroom and closed the door. I didn't really have to go. I just wanted to be by myself. I could still hear them talking though, because they were getting pretty loud.

"Helen, it must be hard for Cassie. She's been carrying this stuff around with her for a long time."

"Well, it's hard for me too, Les! I don't know what to think. How serious do you think this is?"

"I think it's very serious," Daddy answered. "He's practically raped her! And he may even be playing some sick little games with Robbie and his own kids."

"Oh, Les. Fred doesn't seem the type to be doing those kinds of things. Do you think she imagined any of this?"

"I'm sorry you were at another one of your damned meetings tonight, Helen. If you'd heard Cassie and Lisa, I don't think you'd be taking this so lightly."

"Well, Lisa's very level headed. But you know how Cassie idolizes that family. Is it possible she was so infatuated with Fred that she misinterpreted his friendliness?"

I couldn't believe my ears. I'd been afraid Mom might get mad at me, like it was my fault or something, or that maybe she'd never let me leave the house again. But I'd never once thought she might not believe me. I felt all hot inside, like I would explode.

Telling

I went running into the kitchen, stopped right in front of Mom and screamed at her, "You want to know why I never tell you anything? That's why! You don't even believe me when I do. You don't even trust me! You think I'm some kind of stupid liar, and I never even lie to you!"

"Cassie," she started, but I didn't stop to hear anything.

"Why don't you call your precious Lisa and ask her what happened. You can believe her, she's so 'level headed'," I mocked.

"Cassie … " She started again, reaching toward me.

"You're the one who kept making me go babysit, anyway. You don't even care! You probably wish that Fred Sloane would kidnap me! I hate you!"

Mom drew back her arm and slapped me hard across the mouth.

Daddy was off his chair and between us in an instant. "That's enough!" he said. "You owe your mother an apology, Cassie."

"Why? She's the one who hit me!" I said, crying. Daddy was holding on to me with one hand and Mom with the other. He led us into the living room and sat us on the couch. Mom's face was red and it looked like she wanted to hit me again. I wished she would.

"It's true," I said to Daddy. "She likes Robbie better than she likes me, and she never listens to anything I say to her. She even likes Lisa better than she likes me, and Lisa's not even her own kid."

I wanted to tell Mom I hated her again, but when I looked over at her, she was crying. I didn't hate her anymore.

"You don't really believe that, do you, Cassie? That I like Robbie and Lisa better than I like you?"

"Sometimes it seems like it," I told her, sobbing and trying to catch my breath.

"You know, Cassie, it's hard for me sometimes, too. I don't always think you like me very much, either."

"Yeah, but I never call you a liar."

"Your mother didn't call you a liar, Cassie. Let's not make things worse than they are," Daddy said.

"It's not that I think you're a liar, Cassie. It's just that I can hardly believe Fred Sloane would do such a thing. I'm shocked, that's all."

She asked me to go through the whole story again. I did. They talked about what to do. Just before we went to bed, Mom put her arms around me.

"I'm sorry, Cassie. I don't want to fight with you."

"I'm sorry too, Mom."

I didn't want to think about what would happen next. Daddy said something had to happen with Fred Sloane. He couldn't get away with the things he'd been doing to me.

8

Daddy was sitting on the edge of my bed. He rubbed his hand across my cheek. "Come on, Cassie. Ride down to the bank with me. I have to drop some papers off."

"Just let me sleep," I whined.

"No. I need your company. Come on." His voice was gentle, but I could tell he meant for me to go with him, and it was no use arguing. I used to go in to his work with him a lot on Saturdays. We'd go to the bank for a while, and I'd play like I was a teller and fool around with the computer in Daddy's office. Then we'd go out to breakfast at Clifton's Cafeteria. But it had been a long time since we'd done that.

We'd been driving on the freeway for about ten minutes when I realized my dad hadn't said a word. I was so numb, I'd hardly noticed that he wasn't talking at all. At home he watches TV a lot, but in the car he always wants to talk. I wondered if he was feeling numb, too.

We parked in the underground lot and took the escalator to the patio of First Business Bank. It's one of those banks that has a lot of glass and the inside looks like the lobby of some fancy hotel. Dad handed the security guard his special identification card, even though Mr. Mullins, the guard, knows him real well. Big banks have big rules.

"Good morning, Mr. Jenkins. Can this be Cassie?"

Mr. Mullins looked at me, smiling. "What a young lady

you are now, Cassie. I wouldn't have recognized you without your dad here."

"Hi, Mr. Mullins," I mumbled. I always used to like Mr. Mullins, but I didn't want to hear any of that "young lady how you've grown" talk right then.

He opened the double doors for us and locked them behind us again. No one else was inside, and Dad took my hand and led me over to a bench at the edge of the big planter area. I thought how much bigger the rubber trees were than when I last saw them. Dad sat down on the bench and motioned for me to sit down beside him. When I did, he put his arm around my shoulder and pulled me close to him. He was quiet for a moment, then he said, "I thought about you all last night, after I went to bed. I was so angry when I heard what Sloane had been doing to you that, at first, I wasn't exactly thinking about you. You know?"

I nodded my head.

"I love you a lot, Cassie. I'm so sorry about what's happened with Sloane. I keep thinking, what a terrible introduction to sex you've had. My heart aches." He looked at me for a long time. Then he put his other arm around me, too, and pulled me against his chest. It was nothing like the way Fred Sloane had pulled me to him.

"I'm so ashamed that you couldn't come to me for help— that you had to turn to Lisa. I feel so guilty—like such a failure. But I want you to know that I'm with you, on your side, no matter what. I'll take care of you. Everything's going to be all right."

He was hugging me real tight. I knew he meant what he was saying. It was such a relief to me, to feel safe, that it felt like something inside of me started to come loose. I began to cry, but I was crying with my whole body. I was shaking and crying and gasping for air all at the same time.

"Shhh, shhh," Daddy said, stroking my hair and rocking me back and forth. "It's all right. It's going to be all right."

He kept rocking me like that and holding me tight, and when I finally stopped gasping and shaking, I knew that Daddy was crying, too. I could feel his tears in my hair, where he'd kind of buried his head, and I felt him catch his breath.

I reached my arms around his chest and held on even tighter. I didn't know which one of us was doing the rocking then, but I felt a kind of layer lift, like one of the covers I'd buried myself under, only this was maybe a layer of numbness.

Finally Daddy asked, "Why didn't you tell me?"

"I don't know. I was afraid to, I guess."

He reached behind him and took a handful of rich, moist dirt from the planter and let it sift through his fingers.

"Do you remember how you used to play in this dirt when the building was brand new? You'd make little roads and houses with pebbles, and be filthy in five minutes. And then when I was finished and ready to take you to eat, I'd carry you into the men's room and stand you in one of the sinks and practically give you a bath. And you loved drying off with the warm air nozzle. Things were easier when you were three."

"I guess they were. I liked it here on Saturdays."

He told me about when I was born, some stuff I'd heard before, but it seemed almost like a new story, the way he told it then.

"I was there when you were born, Cassie. I wore a sterile gown and mask, and I coached your mother so she'd breathe right. I saw you emerge, head first, like some kind of miracle. As soon as I saw your head, I was pulling for you. In my heart I was saying 'breathe, breathe, move, move, live, live,' and in an instant you were gasping and crying and moving your legs and arms around. You were all red and wrinkly and beautiful. I was filled with the purest kind of love I'd ever experienced. I wanted to shout my thanks to God, or the Great Life Force, or whatever was behind this grand and glorious design that brought you to me. The nurse cleaned you and wrapped you in a soft, light blanket, and put you in my arms. I held you close to me and swore to be the best father to you that a girl could ever have."

He shook his head slowly, looking at me, and then put his hands over his face and began to cry again. I leaned as close to him as I could get. I'd never seen him cry before that day, except once a long time ago when his friend Victor had been killed in a car wreck.

I put my hand on his back and felt him hold his breath and let go, hold his breath and let go, the way I do sometimes when I'm trying to stop crying.

"When I first held you, I thought of all the mistakes my father had made, and I knew I would never make those mistakes with you. You were so helpless and tiny and perfect. I loved your knuckles—they were tiny and fragile but they functioned without a hitch. Your toes and fingers, knees and nose and little puckering ready-to-suck mouth - I was in awe of it all. I loved watching you grow, learn to focus your eyes, use your hands, laugh. That first laugh—you were a wonder to me, Cassie." He looked at me and smiled. "You are still a wonder to me."

I smiled back. It was our first smile of the day. But hearing Daddy talk like that made me wish I could be a baby again. I told him so.

"Yeah, I know. Sometimes I think it would be easier to be a kid again, too. But we've all got to grow up. It would be turning our backs on the gift of life not to grow up, or not to stay grown up once we get there. That's not for us, Cassie."

"Daddy?"

"Yes, Cassie?"

"I'm glad you know."

"I wish it had been sooner," he said. "That's something else I thought about all last night. I don't think parents should have to be mind readers, but I sure should have picked up on your clues."

"What do you mean?" I asked.

"Well, like why were you suddenly wearing that jacket, zipped up all the way to the top, no matter how hot it was outside? And why were you suddenly so reluctant to babysit? And why were you, who had always been Miss Independence personified, all of a sudden dependent on Lisa? There were lots of hints that things weren't quite right with you, and I didn't even ask. I was so caught up in my own little world, work mostly, that I was not being much of a father. I was not remembering any of my promises to that precious gift of life.

I think that's what's happening with Mom, too. I know she loves you. We've all got to work on this together."

"But Mom's so hard to talk to. And she's always bossing me around. And I really do think she likes Robbie and Lisa better than me."

"Maybe it seems that way, Cassie. But I know she loves you a lot."

"She sure doesn't act like it," I said. I was almost crying again.

"You'll see. Give her a chance. She feels as badly about all of this as I do. We talked for a long time last night."

I didn't say anything. I felt sorry about the things I'd said to my mom. But even though we'd sort of made up last night, I wasn't sure things were really okay with her.

"Are you hungry, Cassie?" Daddy asked. "I am, and I'm tired, too. Let's go get some breakfast."

I stood up. My legs were practically asleep from sitting there so long. We must have been there for about two hours on the same bench. Daddy looked at me and laughed. "As usual, you look a mess after hanging around this planter."

He picked me up and put me over his shoulder and started walking to the men's room. Just as we got to the door he put me down, laughing. I noticed he didn't look so fresh and neat himself. He looked tired, and older than I usually thought of him as being. His face was still kind of puffy. I put my arms around him.

"You really are the best father I could ever have," I told him. He just held me for a long time.

When I came out of the restroom, we both looked a lot better. It had been a hard, hard morning, but I somehow felt lighter and fresher, younger maybe, than I had since the whole Fred Sloane thing had begun. I knew there were more hard times ahead with Mom, and then what about the next time Angie called for a babysitter? But I believed my dad, that things would somehow be okay.

9

When I saw all that food lined up in the cafeteria, I realized I was starving. I started loading up my tray—jello salad, potato salad, spaghetti with meatballs. I wasn't even thinking, just taking whatever looked good to me. I was reaching for a baked potato when Dad said, "Remember, your favorite dessert awaits you at the end of the line."

I left the baked potato.

"You can always come back for more if you're still hungry after you've finished that 18,000 calorie meal."

I smiled at him. I felt closer to him than I had for a long time. I didn't even mind hearing the same old "You can always come back for more" talk.

The food was great. And I did go back for a baked potato, with lots of butter. And I ate it all. There's nothing like about thirty-six hours without food to make everything taste totally delicious. I probably could have even eaten a helping of Mom's yucky chicken enchilada casserole.

"I talked with Robbie this morning, before I came to drag you out of bed," Daddy said, as I took my last bite of chocolate cake. "I asked him if Fred ever touched him in private places, or in ways he didn't like."

"What did he say?" I asked, feeling the cake go dry in my mouth.

"Well, I asked him a lot of specific questions, and I'm

convinced that Fred wasn't messing with Robbie."

I felt another of those heavy, invisible layers of fear floating away.

"I think we should call the police and tell them what's been going on," Daddy said.

The layer of fear hovered then, near me, but it was nothing like before.

We got home about 12:30. Mom and Robbie were at the breakfast bar eating tuna sandwiches.

"Want some?" Mom asked as we walked in.

"No thanks," Dad said, laughing. "Cassie and I just ate. And ate. And then Cassie ate some more."

"Oh, good. I'm glad you've got your appetite back," Mom said, smiling at me.

Daddy looked at Robbie, who had a pitted olive over each finger, and said to Mom, "Let's talk some, after Robbie goes outside."

Robbie began to eat the olives, very slowly, starting with the one on his pinky finger, left hand, and then taking one from his right hand pinky.

"Hurry up, Robbie," Dad said, "so you can go play."

"I don't want to play," Robbie said, through his mouthful of olives.

"Oh, come on, Robbie. You've been telling me all morning about how you wanted to build a fort out back. Now's your chance," Mom said.

"But now I want to stay with you guys. I want to hear your talk."

Daddy picked Robbie up off the stool, sat him on the floor, and told him to leave the kitchen. He could go outside and play, go into the den and watch TV, or he could go take a nap.

"Nap!" Robbie said defiantly. As he stomped out of the room he yelled, "How come you guys get to have a talk and I don't?"

"Robbie ..." Daddy said, in a way that meant no questions asked.

As soon as Robbie was out of hearing range, Daddy said, "I think I need to talk with Sloane, Helen. What do you think?"

"You mean you just handle it? Instead of involving the police?"

"Yeah, or at least talk to him before we call the police. Just let him know we're on to him. Maybe that's all it would take."

I was relieved. The thought of calling the police on Fred Sloane really scared me.

Mom started cleaning up the dishes. "I don't know, Les. You can't predict how he'll react. What if he gets violent?"

"He's a bully and a coward or he wouldn't be picking on twelve-year-old girls to begin with. He won't stand up to a man! Besides, I wish he would swing at me. It would give me an excuse to do what I most want to do!"

Daddy's voice was getting louder, and his face was set hard.

"Les, please," Mom said. "You can't mean that. You're the one who always tells Robbie not to hit back, that fighting never solves anything. You're talking crazy."

"Oh, it won't come to that. I tell you, he's a coward," Daddy said, more calmly. "I want you to go with me, Cassie."

"Why?" I squeaked.

"Because I want him to know that we're together. I want you to be there in case he thinks he can lie his way out of this."

"But Daddy," I pleaded. "Please don't make me go."

My stomach was tight and I could feel all of the morning's food rolling around inside.

"Listen to me, Cassie. Maybe if you never went over there again that would solve the immediate problem. But what about the next babysitter, or the next? What if Fred gets more and more aggressive and ends up raping some girl?"

"Dad's right, Cassie. Fred has to know that he can't get away with that kind of thing, that people know about him," Mom said.

"But Daddy … "

"No buts, Cassie. I know it's hard for you, but it must be done. I'm going to call Fred right now and tell him we want to come talk with him."

Daddy went into the den to call. I was so nervous, my hands were all sweaty and my stomach felt awful. I went into the bathroom and splashed cold water on my face. It didn't help. When I came back out, Daddy was in the kitchen again. "No one was home, Cassie," he told me. "We'll try again later."

I hoped they'd be gone for a month, but I was pretty sure they wouldn't.

"Anyone home? Come on, we know you're in there."

As usual Aunt Trudy started talking before she even really got inside the house. Robbie came running out of his bedroom at the sound of her voice, and she came barreling into the kitchen, with Lisa sort of dragging along behind her. She took one look at us and stopped.

"I can see you've had a nice morning," she said. "Are we close to the last and final round?"

"Trudy, this is serious," Daddy said.

"I know, Les."

"It is, Trudy," Mom said.

Aunt Trudy went over to Mom and put her arms around her. She looked down at Mom. "I know, little sister. I know. But how serious can you be all at once? You're probably all exhausted right now. Am I right? I know I'm right. If you're not exhausted, you should each rush to the nearest plastic surgeon because you have some very bad face problems."

I laughed. That's one of the things I liked about Aunt Trudy. She could always make me laugh. I could feel us all start to relax a little.

"I told Lisa I'd drop her and Cassie at the Old Bijou. They're doing a Woody Allen festival. These girls need a little good, clean fun in their lives, huh, Cassie?"

She winked at me and gave out with this window-shattering laugh of hers. As soon as Aunt Trudy suggested a movie, I knew that was exactly what I needed—just to get away from the whole thing for a while.

"Woody Allen?" Mom frowned. "Not exactly wholesome family fare, would you say?"

I was already on my way to take a quick shower and get cleaned up. I could tell that my parents would go along with Aunt Trudy's idea. They almost always did. I'd hardly even looked at Lisa. I felt sort of strange with her.

After my shower I felt a lot better. By the time I was ready, everyone was out on the patio drinking iced tea. Robbie was working on his fort in the backyard and Lisa was trying to chin herself on the old clothesline pole.

Mom came over to me and kissed me on the forehead. "Things aren't so bad, Cassie. It will all work out," she said, smiling.

I wasn't really over the fight we'd had the night before. I could see that Mom was trying to be nice to me though.

Lisa dropped from the clothesline pole, her hands red with rust. She washed her hands with the garden hose, dried them on Robbie's shirt, and ran off to the car. Robbie was concentrating so hard on fixing the door to his fort that he didn't even notice he'd been used as a towel.

On the way to the movie, Aunt Trudy said to me, "You've got to talk with your mom some more, Cassie."

"Yeah, but it's hard," I told her.

"You've got to give her a chance," Aunt Trudy said.

We were about five blocks from the movie theater when she pulled into the parking lot of some church.

"Mommm," Lisa whined. "We're going to be late if you don't hurry up. Why are we stopping here?"

"This will only take a minute. We're going to play a little game," Aunt Trudy said.

"Oh, no," Lisa moaned. "Not one of your little games. We'll miss the first part of the movie."

Aunt Trudy ignored Lisa's protests.

"Cassie, I want you to pretend you're the mother, and I'm going to pretend to be you. Start asking me the same kind of questions your mother asked you when you got home last night."

They must have been talking about our fight while I was getting ready to go. It was kind of embarrassing to me, to think they'd all been talking like that. And it didn't sound like any game I wanted to play, either.

Lisa said, "You'd better just do it and get it over with, or we'll never get to the movie."

Aunt Trudy was turned clear around in the driver's seat, facing me.

"Okay," I said.

"Try to make it realistic now," Aunt Trudy urged.

I took a deep breath and started. "Why didn't you tell me? What's wrong with you? What did he do?" I said, trying to sound like my mom.

Aunt Trudy just sat there looking at me. I repeated the questions. This time I was getting warmed up. Aunt Trudy looked down and mumbled something I couldn't even hear.

"Answer me. What did he do, anyway?"

"That stuff," Aunt Trudy mumbled.

"Why didn't you tell me?" I practically yelled at her.

"I dunno," Aunt Trudy said, looking out the car window.

"Come on, Mom," Lisa said. "You made your point. Now take us to the movie like you said you would."

Aunt Trudy still ignored Lisa. "Cassie? What do you think? Did you believe me?"

"I don't know. Maybe not," I said. I could see what she was getting at. I probably hadn't been very convincing with Mom.

"Helen and I played the same game while you were in the shower. Only she was you, and I was pounding her with questions. I think she'll be easier to talk with next time, if you can have a little more to say."

"Trudy, Trudy, Trudy," Lisa called from the backseat. "Please shave off your Dr. Freud beard and take us to the movie!"

Aunt Trudy laughed and started the car again. We got in just at the beginning of "Sleeper." Lisa bought me some Milk Duds and a Coke as a peace offering.

"I'm not mad at you," I told her, while the credits were rolling past on the screen. She gave me one of those flashy, dimple-filled smiles and squeezed my hand.

Woody Allen always makes me laugh. Even if he doesn't say anything, I just like looking at him. Lisa and I got hysterical during "Sleeper." But some of it kind of bothered me, too. I was all mixed up about sex. Before, I'd just been ignorant, but now I was ignorant and mixed up.

I couldn't figure out what part of sex had to do with love, and what part was dirty, and what part was fun. And was it the same for men as for women? I don't mean men like Fred Sloane, but for men like my dad, or Uncle Tom. I couldn't even think of my dad or Uncle Tom doing it, but I guess they did.

Once during the movie I started to worry about the whole Fred Sloane mess, and how I was going to have to go over there with Daddy. And I thought about the awful things I'd said to my mom. But mostly I just laughed at Woody Allen.

Aunt Trudy was waiting for us in front of the theater when the movie was over.

"Oh, no," Lisa moaned. "I hope no one sees her."

She was sitting in her ancient rusted Hillman-Minx, leaning out the window. Her long, purple feather earring was dangling in the breeze and she was puffing on a big, fat cigar. Lisa hated it when her mother smoked cigars in public. I thought it was funny, but Lisa told me I wouldn't think that if Aunt Trudy were my mother and not just my aunt.

As we were leaving, Lisa's boyfriend, Raymond, and his friend, Gregg, came walking up.

"Hi, Lisa," Raymond said. "Have you just seen 'Sleeper'?"

"Yes, and it's hilarious. You'll love it, Raymond. Hi, Gregg," Lisa said.

"Come back in and see it with us," Raymond said.

"We can't. My mother's already here to get us," Lisa said, kind of sheepishly. "C'mon, Cassie," she said, tugging my hand and pulling me in the opposite direction from her mom's car. It was the wrong thing to do, because Aunt Trudy started beeping the horn when she saw us walking away from her.

Raymond turned around at the sound, and when he saw who it was he called, "Hi, Mrs. Torpedo," and laughed.

Her last name's really Toledo, but I guess Raymond liked to joke with Aunt Trudy.

"Hi, Ray Gun," Aunt Trudy yelled, waving her cigar at him and laughing. Lisa just groaned.

On the way home Lisa told Aunt Trudy, "You really do

embarrass me, Mother."

"You'll outgrow it," was all Aunt Trudy said.

I liked other people's arguments better than my own. "You can spend the night with us tonight if you want, Cassie," Aunt Trudy offered. "I talked with your folks about it. Your father's tried to call Fred Sloane several times, but apparently they're gone for the whole day."

"Stay, C.C.," Lisa said. "I want to show you my prom dress, and we can make marshmallow treats."

CHAPTER

10

Uncle Tom was stretched out on the floor, asleep in front of the TV. The Dodgers and Mets were playing, but it must have been a boring game. We stepped over him on our way through the living room and into the kitchen.

Lisa got out the Rice Krispies and marshmallows, and I started greasing the cookie sheet. Aunt Trudy was gathering up dirty dishes and putting them in the sink.

Ever since I was five and Lisa was eight, we would make marshmallow treats at her house. I used to think Lisa was really lucky because she had her own TV in her bedroom, and she could eat whatever she wanted. My mom was always after me to eat my vegetables, and she said sugar was poison and would ruin teeth and make me hyperactive, so I never got marshmallow treats at home. In fact, I never even got Rice Krispies. I either had to eat hot cereal with honey, or some kind of yucky granola with sliced fruit. But at Lisa's we'd make marshmallow treats, get cans of Coke and bags of potato chips, and take our junk food feast into her bedroom, where we would watch some super-violent police show while porking out. My mom used to tell me that Lisa would grow up with bad teeth, and she'd be sure to get acne if she continued to eat such junk. Lisa doesn't even have one cavity though, and the closest thing she's ever had to a zit was when she got a mosquito bit on her chin last summer.

I was glad Aunt Trudy worked it out so I could spend the night. I still felt kind of strange with my mom, and I wanted to put off trying to talk with her. And I for sure didn't want to have to see Fred Sloane. I felt safe for the evening.

"Cassie, when did Fred first start making advances to you?" Aunt Trudy asked.

Oh, no, I thought. All I wanted was junk food, and now I have to get into this again.

"I guess it was a few months ago," I said. I thought back to that first night. It seemed years ago, but it wasn't. "I think it was just after Christmas vacation," I told her.

"Do you think he's pulling that stuff with anyone else?" she asked.

"I don't know."

"Cassie, you know that Lisa did the right thing by telling, don't you?"

I looked at Lisa, who seemed totally engrossed in mixing the Rice Krispies stuff. She didn't look up.

Just then, Uncle Tom called from the living room, "Hey, Trudy, how long you been home? Where's my dinner?"

"You don't need dinner, Gutso," Aunt Trudy said, laughing, as she went into the living room.

She must have wiped her soapy hands on him because I heard Uncle Tom yell, "Hey, I'm pure sugar, remember? If you're not careful I'll melt. Then where would you be?"

They were giggling and scuffling around, and I was glad Aunt Trudy had been momentarily distracted.

Lisa spread the Rice Krispies mixture onto the cookie sheet. I got out the Cokes and potato chips, and we put it all on a big tray and carried it to Lisa's bedroom.

Our houses were a lot alike from the outside. They were the standard California tract, stucco with a shake roof and a little brick planter under the picture window in front, like lots of other houses in Hamilton Heights. Inside though, our house and Lisa's house looked really different.

Aunt Trudy and Uncle Tom had been in the Peace Corps before they got married, and they had all kinds of stuff from Africa and South America. In the living room was a giant weaving, hung from a hunting spear, and in the corner by the fireplace was this gross statue of a woman with huge breasts and other extreme, unnamable features. The statue was about three feet high and it was a shiny black wood carving. It was another cause of embarrassment to Lisa, but Aunt Trudy always told her that Victoria (the name of the statue) was a special fertility goddess, and that Lisa should pay special homage to Victoria every day. She said that without Vicky's help, Lisa would never have been born.

Their kitchen was filled with crude-looking utensils made of wood, and there were all kinds of baskets hanging on the walls, and there was a big fishing net draped from one end of the kitchen to the other. Uncle Tom thought it was a fire hazard because it hung too low over the stove, but Aunt Trudy reassured him it was safe, since she now only used the microwave oven and just kept the gas stove as a decorative piece.

The whole house was like that though, with statues and weavings and pottery pieces, until you entered Lisa's room. It was like something you'd see in Seventeen, bright and crisp and clean. Her walls were white and on her sliding closet doors she had done this graphic design in primary colors. Her desk was painted light blue, the same color as the down comforter on the bed. The windows had these neat canvas shades, with broad stripes, like the stripes on her closet door.

We pulled the TV tray next to the bed, where we both sat cross-legged. We started with Cokes and potato chips.

"I had to tell, C.C. Are you mad at me?"

"No," I told her. I'd already told her that before, but maybe I hadn't been very convincing.

We were both silent for awhile, chewing chips and sipping soda. Then Lisa said, "You should have seen my mom! She was yelling and threatening to go right over to the Sloanes' house and haul him to the police station. She was really outrageous for a while. You know how she can get. Then I was really scared."

"I'm sorry I wouldn't talk to you on the phone," I told her. "I was so confused yesterday. I didn't want to talk to anyone. I didn't even want to think."

"It's okay, C.C. I just don't want you to think I let you down by telling. I really couldn't help it. When I saw Fred yesterday, he was so mean! I thought I'd never seen such an ugly face as his was right then. Remember the night we babysat when he and Angie went to that party? I thought he was kind of handsome then. But I'll never think that again."

"I know," I told her. "I used to think he was kind of handsome, too."

I told Lisa about Thursday night—how Fred had come home early from bowling, and how he had caught me alone in the hall, and how Angie had come home just in time. I didn't tell her about how I had at first let Fred kiss me without fighting him, or how mixed up I'd been about the way my body felt when he started rubbing his hand along my legs. I skipped that part. I guess I was ashamed of those feelings. I told her how scared I was when he just kept pushing at me though, and how relieved I was to hear Angie's car.

"What do you think Angie will say about all this?" Lisa asked.

"Maybe she won't find out," I said.

"How can she not find out? Between your dad and my mom, something's going to come out in the open, and soon!"

I thought about Angie. She'd been a good friend to me. And I thought about some of the grown-up conversations we'd had together. She'd told me about how she and Fred met. He was engaged to someone else at the time, but it had been like love at first sight. They ran off and got married two weeks after their first date. And she told me that everyone in her family thought she was crazy, but she'd never been sorry.

"Angie'll probably hate me now," I said.

"But it's not your fault she's married to a lecher," Lisa said.

"I know. But still, she's my friend."

"Do you think she ever suspected Fred?" Lisa asked.

"No, I don't. I mean, she always talked like Fred was so great."

"Maybe she just wanted to make it seem that way. Maybe she didn't really think he was so great."

I'd never thought about that. It sure seemed to me that she loved Fred, though.

"Do you think Fred's just frustrated because she never gives him any?" Lisa asked.

"Any what?"

"You know. Any sex."

"I don't think that's it," I said. "Angie told me once that Fred was real good to her in bed, and that she never got tired of having him make love to her."

"She told you that?" Lisa said, kind of in a screech.

"Yeah. She told me that a long time ago."

"That's weird, C.C.—a grown-up woman talking to a twelve-year-old about her sex life? I mean, I know you're mature and all, but really, C.C., that's weird!"

"I thought it was kind of interesting," I said.

Our hands were all sticky and we'd consumed nearly the whole batch of gooey stuff. We decided to go for a run. As usual, I was dressed for it in my standard jeans, sweatshirt, and sneakers. We rinsed our hands off at the kitchen sink, yelled our plans to Uncle Tom, and took off running down Lisa's driveway.

We ran all the way down Seventh Street, all the way to Hamilton High School, then we ran three times around the track. We raced the last lap. I won. I can always beat Lisa in a race even though her legs are longer than mine. I can beat her swimming, too. It makes up for her dimples, but not quite. After the last lap, we collapsed on the damp grass in the center of the track.

I love the smell of dewy grass—it smells sweet, and clean. I picked a long blade of grass and held it between my thumbs, blowing a loud, shrill whistle. I did it just for fun, because I like to do a grass whistle and because it always annoys Lisa, who has never managed to get a sound out of any blade of grass held between her thumbs.

On my second whistle, this big golden retriever came running right up to where we were sitting and started licking me all over. The dog's owner, who had also been running laps, came over to retrieve the retriever.

"That's how I whistle for Goldie at home. She's just trying

to be friendly," he explained, attaching a leash to his dog and pulling her away. Lisa was rolling around and laughing.

"That'll teach you to smart off with grass blades," she snorted. "Next time maybe you'll attract an elephant."

It was pretty funny, I guess—me getting all carried away about the dewy, sweet, clean grass, and then being slobbered all over by that grossly affectionate beast.

We started the run back. It was 8:30 and we had definite instructions to be back to Lisa's by 9:00. We were more jogging than running when we passed the Baskin Robbins ice cream place. I glanced inside. I always look in ice cream places. There, sitting at a little wrought iron table and looking like the all-American family, were Angie, Fred, Dorian and Tina.

They didn't see me, but seeing them made me feel strange. A few months ago I would have run in and pulled a chair up to their table. Angie or Fred would have bought me an ice cream and the kids would have fought over who got to sit next to me. We would have laughed and talked and maybe made arrangements for the next time I would babysit. Now it was as if things were kind of frozen. We could never go back to the old way. And something more was going to happen between us. I didn't know exactly what that something would be, but I knew it would be a hard time.

Back at Lisa's house, she took a quick shower, then modeled her prom dress for me. Even though her hair was wet and she was wearing old gym shoes, she looked beautiful. Her dress was long and made from soft, sort of frothy, material. It was a creamy yellow, a color that made her face glow.

"Oh, Lisa. It's beautiful!"

"I know," she said. "It's a perfect dress, isn't it?"

"You look like a model or a movie star or something."

I wondered if I would ever look that good in my whole life. Not that I really wanted to wear a dress like that. It looked uncomfortable to me, like you'd have to be careful all the time not to step on the hem, or sit funny in it, or bend over so far that people could see down the front. But she really did look beautiful.

Telling

After we took the sticky dishes and TV tray out of Lisa's room, and watched TV for a while with Uncle Tom, we crawled into bed under Lisa's down comforter.

In the dark, quiet room Lisa told me, "My mom really does embarrass me sometimes. I can talk to her about almost anything. And she's fun, too, most of the time. But she's so extreme. And then I feel guilty about feeling embarrassed. You know?"

"I know," I told her. "I really feel guilty about my mom sometimes. I said awful stuff to her yesterday, and then when I saw how hurt she looked, I felt bad. She just makes me so angry sometimes though, when she acts like she knows so much, or when it seems like she doesn't trust or believe me."

Lisa said, "My mom says that moms always feel guilty, too. Maybe that's just how it has to be."

"It's hard to believe my mom feels guilty about anything," I said.

"Well, you're wrong about that, C.C. While you were getting ready for the movie today, I heard her tell my mom that she felt terrible about fighting with you, and that it was all her fault. She was crying, C.C."

I didn't say anything. I just thought about that for a while. It was probably the first time I'd ever tried to think about how things felt for my mom. I drifted off to sleep, thinking about Mom, and how Daddy said everything was going to be okay. I was tired from the run, and from all the tension and emotion of the day. I'm the kind of person who has an emotional crisis about once every two years. I was really worn out, and I slept so soundly that I couldn't remember where I was when I first woke up in the morning.

11

Daddy picked me up about 10:00 that Sunday morning. In the car on the way home he told me, "I called Fred Sloane this morning. We're going over there at 11:00."

I begged not to go. I felt sick. But he was insistent that we had to see Fred together.

"What about Mom, and Robbie?" I asked him.

He frowned. "I think your mother should go, too. After all, this does involve the whole family. But she doesn't want Robbie to go, and she says she doesn't want to leave him in the house alone. So she's not going. I think it's an excuse to avoid a big scene."

I wished I had been able to come up with my own excuse.

On our way to the Sloanes', Daddy and I held hands. I noticed that both of us had sweaty palms. We walked slowly. I was roasting. I had changed out of my shorts and blouse into jeans, a sweatshirt, and jacket. I zipped my jacket all the way up to my chin. I guess if I had had a suit of armor hanging in my closet, I would have worn it.

We walked in silence until we reached the Sloanes' house. Fred and Angie were pulling weeds in their flowerbeds along the driveway. Angie saw us first as we walked toward them.

"Hi, Les. Hi, Cassie. How nice of you to come see us on

this bright, sunny morning. How about some iced tea?" She smiled at us as she brushed dirt from her hands.

"No thanks, Angie. We just want to talk with your husband for a few minutes," Daddy said, glancing at Fred.

Fred stood up. "You didn't say over the phone what I could do for you, Les. Muffler problems? Need gas for your lawn mower?" Fred smiled a kind of fake smile.

I could see Tina and Dorian playing in their sandbox in the back. My stomach was turning flip-flops.

"It's more serious than muffler problems, Fred. Maybe we should talk inside."

Fred backed up a little. He looked first at my father, then at me.

"No, we can talk out here," Fred said. "It can't be all that serious, can it?"

"Suit yourself," Daddy said.

"Of course you can come in, Les, if you want," Angie said. She looked at Fred with a kind of puzzled expression. "Maybe we'd all be more comfortable inside. Don't you think?"

Fred's face was set hard. "I said we could talk out here."

Angie nodded. I felt sorry for her. The four of us stood there for a minute. I wanted to turn and run away, or faint, or anything to avoid the inevitable. But I stood there, frozen, still clutching my father's sweating hand.

"Well, there's no need to beat around the bush then," Daddy said, looking straight at Fred. "Cassie tells me you've been making sexual advances to her for some time now."

"WHAT!" Fred screamed. "You've got to be out of your mind!" His face was red and he was looking right at me. Angie just sort of gasped and moved closer to Fred. Daddy seemed real calm.

"No, Fred. I don't think either of us is out of our minds."

"Shit," Fred sneered. "You don't know what the hell you're talkin' about, man. Sexual advances! This kid of yours must have a hell of an imagination. I've patted her on the shoulder a few times. And I lifted her down from the back of my brother's pick-up truck—along with Dorian and Tina, of course. That's the extent of my 'sexual advances' to your daughter."

"What Cassie described to me was not shoulder pats, Fred. It was more like having your hands all over her body, and forcing your tongue into her mouth, and generally trying to get off on her."

"Oh, come on, Jenkins. You know better than that," Fred said.

Angie put her arm around Fred's waist. She looked at me for a long time. "How could you say such a thing, Cassie? You've been like a daughter to us."

"It's true," I said to her. I could feel my face go hot.

"What's wrong with you?" she asked, softly. She didn't sound angry, like Fred, just hurt. "I knew you kind of liked Fred, but this ... "Angie stared at me with disbelief, then she turned to my father. "You know, Les, an adolescent crush can cause strange fantasies," she said.

"Yeah, I know that, Angie. And I also know that your husband has been going after my daughter, and that's no fantasy!"

"You got it all wrong, Buddy," Fred said. "Your daughter comes around here, hangin' around me. She's just telling you what she wishes had happened. You're lucky it was me she was playin' up to. You better watch her or someone not as nice as me'll have her knocked up in no time." He looked at me with a nasty half grin. "She's a ripe little peach," he said.

Angie drew away from Fred, looking at him.

"Well, it's true, Angie. Hey, you know that yourself."

Angie nodded. She was crying. So was I. I felt Daddy's hand tighten in mine. Then he let go of my hand and stepped closer to Fred. They were eye to eye and they both had their fists clenched.

"I'm warning you, you lecherous bastard. Stay away from Cassie."

I'd never heard Daddy call anyone that name, and I'd never heard so much anger in his voice. My hands were shaking. They stood there, fists clenched, mouths tight.

"Get off my property," Fred said. "You're trespassing. You've got this thing all wrong, but you'd better get the hell out of here. Now!"

"Okay, Sloane. But you better believe me when I tell you

that if you ever lay a hand on Cassie again, you'll be in more trouble than you ever thought possible."

Daddy took my hand again and we started down the driveway. He was walking so fast I practically had to run to keep up with him. It was fine with me to run. I wanted out of there.

I was still crying, from being scared, and from missing Angie. I felt bad that she would act like I was dreaming all of that stuff up. I guess I was missing Tina and Dorian, too. Maybe even Fred, strange as that seems. But just a few months ago it seemed like we were practically family, and now things were awful between us.

"That bastard. That bastard," Daddy kept muttering. When we were about a block from home, we met Mom. She had started out toward the Sloanes' house.

"I couldn't stand waiting at home," she said. "You were right, Les. I should have gone over there with you. What happened?" She looked worried.

"That bastard!" Daddy said, then went on to tell her about our meeting. He told her what Angie had said about adolescent fantasies, and how Fred said I only wanted that stuff to happen and that they'd better keep an eye on me.

"Cassie, Fred really did all of those things you told us about, didn't he?" Mom asked. I could see she was having her doubts.

Before I even had a chance to answer, Daddy said, "You wouldn't ask that question if you'd been with us just now and seen Fred Sloane. He almost had me believing him— not that Cassie was lying, but maybe she had exaggerated or misinterpreted some of his actions. But when he started in on what a ripe little peach she is … I could see it all over his face. That bastard! He's been after her for sure."

I was relieved. For a minute, with Angie, I started to think that maybe I had made it all up. I mean, Angie and Fred had been pretty convincing. And no one else had ever really seen any of that stuff with their own eyes. But now that Daddy had seen Fred that way, I had confidence that I really did know what I was talking about.

When we got home, Robbie was sitting on the front porch in his Mickey Mouse hat and his swimming trunks.

"I thought I told you to stay inside until I got back, Robbie," Mom said.

"I was scared of the burglars."

"What burglars?" Mom asked.

"The ones I heard trying to get into the house. They were making noises outside your bedroom window, Mom."

Robbie always hears burglars. He used to hear monsters, but now it's just burglars.

"I really did, Mom. I know you don't believe me but I really did this time." Robbie's voice was getting louder and higher with each word.

"Okay, Robbie, let's go look," Dad said.

I can't believe how many times they have looked for burglars and monsters to reassure Robbie.

Just as Mom and I got to the front door, the phone started ringing. Mom ran to the kitchen to answer it. It was Angie. I couldn't tell what the conversation was because Mom just kept saying maybe, and I don't think so, and things which gave me no clue.

Daddy and Robbie had completed the burglar search and Robbie was flopped in front of the TV watching "The Wizard of Oz."

Mom came into the den. "Angie called to say she was terribly concerned about Cassie, and to suggest that Cassie see a psychologist."

"Cassie see a psychologist? The one who needs a psychologist is her lecher of a husband!" Dad yelled. "And maybe she ought to see one, too, for being married to that scum."

"What's a lecher, Daddy?" Robbie asked, distracted from the tornado scene by Daddy's yelling.

"Oh, just a person who's not very nice," Daddy said.

"Who's a lecher?" Robbie asked.

"No one you know, Robbie. Hey look, Toto's found Dorothy again."

"It is too someone I know, I bet," Robbie said. But he turned back to Dorothy and Toto.

Daddy walked back out to the kitchen with Mom and I followed.

"So what else did she say?" he asked in a lowered voice.

"She said Cassie needed help distinguishing between her sexual fantasies and the real world, and that it was lucky for Cassie that she chose to accuse someone as understanding as Fred."

When I heard that, it wasn't so hard for me to think about losing Angie as a friend. I mean, how could she ever have been my friend, or even known me, if she believed I was such a liar?

"What a bunch of bull," Daddy said.

"I felt kind of sorry for Angie on the phone just now," Mom said.

"Oh, I know," Daddy said, his face softening a little. "She's in a bad spot, too. And even Fred—why is he like that? He can't be very happy right now, do you think?"

They talked for a long time about the Sloanes and what to do next. Mostly I just listened, unless they asked me a question. It all seemed more important than I wanted it to be. I was beginning to feel a little more relaxed with my mom, though.

We'd probably been in the kitchen for about an hour when I heard the doorbell. Now what, I thought, but it was only Mandy.

"Hey, Robbie. What's the haps?" she asked, walking through the den and into the kitchen. Robbie didn't even look up. The Tin Man was singing "If I Only Had a Heart," Robbie's favorite part except for where the Wicked Witch gets her just desserts.

"Hi, everybody," Mandy said as she crossed the kitchen and opened the refrigerator door. "What have you got to feed a poor starving orphan? Francine never buys groceries anymore."

Mandy started poking around, looking in bowls of leftovers, then pulled out the milk carton and poured herself a glass.

Mom used to get mad at Mandy for making herself so at home in our refrigerator, but she said she could never stay mad long enough to make it worth her while.

"Hey, Cassie, there's a party at Julia's house tonight. Wanna go?"

"On Sunday night?" Daddy said.

"Oh, you know, Jenks, it'll be over by 9:30. It's really just a few kids getting together."

"I don't even like parties that much," I reminded Mandy.

"Yeah, but this will be different," she said. She rolled her eyes at my parents and then said, "Come on, Cassie, let's go out on the patio." Mandy practically pushed me out the door. With the door closed behind us, Mandy started jumping up and down, clapping her hands and squealing at me, "Guess what? Guess what?"

"What?" I guessed.

"Guess who called me. Oh, it's who I always wanted to have call me. Guess who, Cassie."

My mind was still on the hassles of the day, but I tried to go along with Mandy.

"Who?" I guessed.

"Eric!" she shrieked. "You know, Eric! Eric who I've loved since the fifth grade and who never even looks at me. He called! He wanted to know if I would be at Julia's party. He said he hoped I would! I'm so happy!"

Mandy's face was all red, and her eyes were kind of glittery. She sat down on the lawn swing and pulled me down beside her. "Wait until you hear this part, though. Eric called me back about fifteen minutes later and asked if you were going to Julia's party. He said Jason wanted to know, but he was too shy to call you himself. You've got to go, Cassie. It'll be so cool! Me and Eric and you and Jason."

"I don't even know if I like Jason," I told her. "And I know I don't like parties. I mean, everyone just stands around and eats and I've already eaten. And I never know what to say to anybody."

"But Cassie, it'll be different with a boyfriend. Please go. Francine might not even let me go if you don't go. She doesn't know Julia, and she always thinks you're so sensible. Please?"

I did sort of think Jason was cute. And I didn't want to let Mandy down. It didn't sound like much fun. Why would it be more fun worrying about what to say to Jason than it would have been worrying about what to say to people in general? It might be good to get out of the house for a while. Everything felt so heavy here.

"Well, okay. I guess."

Mandy grabbed me and hugged me. "You're such a pal! I knew you'd do it. I told Eric I was sure you'd be there!"

I wished I felt as happy about it as Mandy did. The most enthusiasm I could gather was to tell myself that maybe it would be okay, and anyway it wouldn't last very long.

"Let's go see what you're going to wear. It's kind of like a first date. I'm not telling Francine that Eric called, though. She'd probably think we were going to some kind of orgy or something."

We walked back through the kitchen. Mom and Dad were still sitting there talking.

"Is it okay if I go to the party with Mandy tonight?" I asked.

"I don't know, Cassie," Mom said. "You've had a pretty difficult day. Maybe you'd better stay home this evening."

"On the other hand," Daddy said, "maybe it would do you good to get out for a while."

Mom didn't look convinced, but she said, "Well, I guess you can go. But you'll have to leave the party by 9:30 at the very latest. I'll bet you're behind with your schoolwork. In fact, I'll come get you right at 9:30. Tell your mother I can take you home, too, Mandy."

"Thanks, Mrs. Jenkins," Mandy said.

We went to my room, and Mandy started sorting through my closet.

"These jeans look best on you," she told me, pulling out my only pair of designer jeans. Mom bought them for me last Christmas, even though I preferred Levi's.

"And this blouse, Cassie. This is great."

Telling

She tossed me a white blouse that was all lacy at the neck and sleeves. It wouldn't be as comfortable as a sweatshirt, but I went along with Mandy's planning. I drew the line at using blush and lipstick though. I thought it was stupid to put all that stuff on your face.

"Just try a little, Cassie. You'll look great, and no one will even know you're wearing it."

But I wouldn't be convinced. I went to the party unblushed.

We were the first ones there. Mandy and Julia giggled while I wished I had stayed at home. Then other kids started coming in. When Eric and Jason arrived they stayed on the opposite side of the room and didn't even look at us. There were only about twelve kids there, so it was easy to feel self-conscious. Finally though, Julia and Todd started dancing. Then Eric and Jason walked over to us. Eric said to Mandy, "Wanna dance?" and they were out in the middle of the floor, leaving me and Jason to stare at each other.

"Wanna dance?" Jason mumbled.

"I don't know how," I said.

"Me neither," Jason said. We stood there.

"Wanna try?"

"Okay," I said.

We both kind of stood in the middle of the floor, watching, and then we started moving around, trying to look like everyone else. It was more fun than I thought it would be. Then someone put on some slow music. Jason looked as worried as I felt, but he had one arm around my waist and took my hand in his other hand. Everyone else was dancing real close, but the only parts of our bodies that were touching were hand to hand, hand to waist, hand to shoulder. Jason's hand was kind of damp, and it felt small, almost breakable. I guess I'd never even touched a boy my own age. Daddy's hands felt strong and dependable. And Fred Sloane's hands felt rough and forceful. When I noticed that Jason was nervous, I was more relaxed. He seemed safer, and less of a mystery to me.

When we left the dance floor we went to get some punch, then sat down on the couch by the fireplace.

"You weren't at school Friday," Jason said.

"No, I wasn't," I agreed. Then we both just sat there, sipping our punch. After this eternally long silence, I finally thought of something to say.

"Want some potato chips?"

"Yeah, let's get some," Jason said. So we walked back to the table. I managed to sneak a look at the clock. It was only 9:00. I hoped Mom's watch would be a little bit fast. I looked over at Mandy and Eric, standing by the window. They were talking and laughing. I wondered how Mandy did it. Jason and I hardly said anything more until he said good night to me as we were leaving. But the next morning, in my locker, there was this note that said, "I like you," and it was signed "J.B." for Jason Bartel.

12

I was glad to be at school Monday morning. So much had happened to me in such a short time, I felt all confused. Only four days ago, Thursday night, Fred Sloane had come home early from bowling and cornered me. I hadn't even figured out how I felt about all of that when I had to try to explain it to Daddy, and then to Mom. It seemed as if what had been a big secret for months had just exploded, and all of a sudden lots of people were involved. Every time I looked at Mom or Daddy now, it was like they were seeing me differently, maybe worrying more, or wondering what other secrets I had. Anyway, at school I could just coast through the day. I was coasting first period when I heard Marlow call my name. Everyone was looking at me. I felt my face get hot.

"Daydreaming, Cassie?" Mr. Marlow asked. "Perhaps you could answer my question now."

Mandy poked me in the back. "Indirect object," she whispered.

"Indirect object," I told Marlow.

"That's correct, Cassie. Would you explain your answer, please?"

Explain the answer! I didn't even know what question we were on. My face just got hotter and hotter. Finally Marlow said, "Well, Mandy, how about if you explain Cassie's answer for her?"

On the way to gym Mandy started talking about what a jerk Marlow was for putting people on the spot like that.

"I guess I just wasn't listening," I said.

Mandy laughed. "Weren't listening? You were not only out to lunch, you were out to breakfast and dinner, too."

Good old Mandy. I could always depend on her to give me an honest opinion.

"You were real quiet last night at the party, too," she said.

"I never know what to say. I'm always quiet at parties."

"Yeah, but not that quiet. It was okay, I guess, because Jason really likes you." Then she went on and on about how great Eric was—how cute, how much fun, how he said he'd call her that night.

We walked into the gym and got our graying gym clothes out of our locker. My blouse didn't smell very good, but neither did Mandy's.

"You really are kind of quieter than usual. Is everything all right?"

"I guess so," I said. "It's just that a lot happened over the weekend."

"Yeah," Mandy agreed. "What a weekend! I filled three pages in my diary just last night. Wasn't it a great party?"

"It was better than I thought it'd be," I told Mandy.

She looked at me suspiciously. "So what else happened to you over the weekend?"

"Oh, just some stuff with my folks. Come on, we'd better get out on the field before the bell rings."

We jogged out to the softball diamond. Ms. Strobel wasn't there yet, so we flopped down on the grass to wait for roll call.

"I don't mean to be nosy, Cassie, but we are best friends, aren't we?"

I gave Mandy our secret handshake, invented by us in the third grade, and smiled. She crossed her eyes, pulled on her ears, and stuck out her tongue. I pretended to thread a needle, then began sewing my fingers together. We laughed and snorted and threw grass at each other. I know Mandy and I will always be best friends because we can always act like little kids together.

At lunchtime we took our sandwiches and sat on the front

steps of the school. Eric eats there sometimes, and Mandy wanted to just happen to be there in case he showed up.

I took my cucumber and cheese sandwich on sprouted wheat bread from my sack lunch, and opened my thermos of low fat milk. Mandy took her bologna and catsup sandwich on white crustless bread and her can of soda. I thought of Mom and her theories of health. Mandy ate whatever she wanted, just like Lisa did, and neither one of them was ever sick, or had pimples, or anything. Not that I was really hungry for a bologna and catsup sandwich, but I did wish for a Hostess Twinkie in my lunch sometimes.

"So what's happening at your house?" Mandy asked.

"My parents are all upset about something that happened to me."

"What?"

"It's kind of a secret. You have to promise not to tell anyone."

"I'm not a blabbermouth," she said, then admitted, "Well, yeah, I am a blabbermouth, but not with secrets."

"And you can't let my parents know that you know," I told her.

"I won't," she promised. She took the Twinkie out of her lunch bag, broke it in half and handed half to me. I wanted to tell her. I just didn't know where to start.

I remembered the time in the fourth grade when Mandy and I were walking from school to a Bluebird meeting and she started crying. She told me her father and mother were getting a divorce, and her father wouldn't be living with them anymore, and how unhappy she was. And I remembered how once when Robbie was only about two and seemed to be the only one my parents cared about, I told Mandy I wished Robbie would get sick and die, and she stayed my friend anyway, even after she knew how mean I really was.

"You know the Sloanes who live near us?" I asked.

She nodded. "Sure. I even babysat at their house once last summer, when you were away. Remember?"

"Well, Mr. Sloane, Fred, was getting all weird with me."

Once I started it was easy to tell Mandy the whole story. Well, almost the whole story. I couldn't exactly tell her about all my feelings because I was still confused about some stuff. But I told her about everything that happened, including the awful fight with Mom, and Angie saying I needed to see a psychologist.

Mandy was quiet for a while. Then she told me, "Something kind of strange happened the time I babysat there, too."

"What?"

Mandy frowned. "It happened so fast, it's almost like it didn't happen at all, but now I really wonder," she said.

"So what was it?"

"Well … when Mr. Sloane took me home, he got out of the car and walked me to my door. He held money out, to pay me, and when I reached for it he dropped it. We both bent to pick it up, and then he reached out and sort of brushed his hand across my, you know … my chest. And then he turned around and walked away. I was so surprised, I just stood there. And then I thought, 'This didn't happen.' I mean it was so strange."

"I bet it happened for sure," I told Mandy. "But I kind of thought that at first, too, that it couldn't really be happening."

"He must be some kind of creep," Mandy said. "I hate to babysit anyway, so I knew I'd never go back there. I didn't even think about it again 'til just now. What's with him anyway, I wonder?"

"Hi, Mandy." It was Eric. "I looked for you out at the lunch tables," he smiled. Mandy flashed her winning smile back at him.

"Cassie and I came out here for a little private conversation," she said in her most sophisticated voice.

"Well come on, I'll walk you to class," he told her.

"To be continued," Mandy said to me. "I'll see you after school."

We were going in opposite directions, so I picked up our trash and went off to the science room. It was kind of a surprise to me that Fred had done that to Mandy. I think I sort of felt jealous at first. And then I felt stupid. How dumb I had been to think maybe he was in love with me. I remembered how I had been almost flattered that he was interested in me in a way that had to do with sex. I'm so unsexy! God, was I ever stupid!

I felt a gentle tug on my hair and turned to look behind me. It was Jason. "Get my note?" he asked.

I smiled at him. "Thanks, Jason," I said. That's all I could think of to say.

"You're welcome," he answered. He smiled back, showing a mouthful of metal, then turned and walked back down the hall.

On my way home from school that afternoon I thought about the time I'd gone to Disneyland with the Sloanes. It was last summer, when Tina was three. Angie had invited me so I could help with Tina and Dorian on some of the rides. And she told me it would be more fun for her and Fred too, if I went along.

In the evening, when we were all tired, we'd gone on the Pirates of the Caribbean ride. We sat in the first row of the boat, Angie on the outside edge. Then there was Tina, then me, then Dorian and then Fred. Tina was frightened by the fake cannonball shots and the fire in the jail, and she buried her head first in Angie's lap and then in mine. Dorian laughed the whole way at everything we saw. We all got hit in the face with a huge splash of water when the boat went down the last waterfall. We were all wet and laughing when we got off, and I felt good to be with them.

At the car, Angie told me to sit in front with Fred so she could get in back with the kids and maybe help them get to sleep. On the long ride back home, Fred asked me about what I thought I'd do when I grew up, and he told me how he first got started in the muffler business. He said he thought I was pretty smart and I should be sure to get a job where I used my brains. Angie had joked with me and told me that if I kept getting prettier and prettier I'd probably end up with some rich man and never have to use my brains.

It seemed like they were really interested in me, and like they really liked me. I wondered, walking home from school, where that time had gone. What happens to good times when the bad times come?

I had been so lost in my thoughts that I hardly realized I was almost home. I had just turned the corner on to Fairview when I heard the roar of a motorcycle behind me, right up on the sidewalk. I jumped to the side. It was Fred. He stopped in front of me, blocking my way with his bike. He got off and stood there, facing me. I started to walk around him, keeping my eyes on the ground, but he took two quick steps and grabbed me. His face was only inches away from mine, and his eyes were hateful.

"You better keep your mouth shut, you little tramp!" he hissed at me. "You come hanging around me, begging me for a little fun, and then when you get your way you go trying to get me in trouble."

He was holding my wrists so tightly I could hardly move. I tried to pull away. "Leave me alone!" I shouted.

He shoved me aside. "I'll leave you alone all right. But you better stop telling lies about me!"

I ran the rest of the way home. I didn't even look back once. He must have come out looking for me. I hated him. What did he mean accusing me of hanging around him, and of lying? He was the one who was lying. And I sure never asked him to come home early from bowling the other night!

Mom was watering the lawn when I came running up the driveway.

"What's your hurry, Cassie? You look a little red in the face."

I dropped my book bag on the driveway and sat down.

"It's Fred Sloane again," I told her. "He came after me over on Fairview Street. He told me to keep my mouth shut, and he called me a tramp." I was choking back tears. Mom came over and sat down next to me.

"Were you afraid, Cassie? Did you think he was going to hurt you, or force himself on you in some way?"

"Not really. It happened so fast, I didn't have time to be scared. He did kind of hurt my wrists when he grabbed me though." I showed Mom my wrists, which were still all red.

"I don't like this at all, Cassie. We're going to have to call the police."

"Oh, Mom. What will they do? Will I have to talk to them? Pretty soon I can go to Grammy's. Let's just wait."

"No, Cassie. This whole thing has gone too far. We can't be sure what Fred will do next. We'll wait for Dad, but we'll have to report this. In the meantime, I don't want you to leave the house."

I was kind of shaky. I went into the den where Robbie was watching "Sesame Street." I sat down next to him.

"Do you like Big Bird, Cassie?" he asked.

"Sure, I like Big Bird."

"Are you in love with Big Bird?" he asked, grinning.

"No. Are you in love with Big Bird?"

"No!" he shrieked, giggling. "I'm in love with Miss Piggy!"

He laughed until his face was all red and he got the hiccups. He thought the dumbest things were hilarious. But as I watched him laughing and hiccupping, I was glad he hadn't gotten sick and died like I wanted him to that time when he was only two years old. And I was very glad Fred Sloane hadn't been all weird with Robbie.

I started on my math homework, but my stomach kept reminding me that there was stuff to be nervous about. Mom had fixed one of my favorite meals, spaghetti with garlic bread and salad, but I wasn't very hungry. We didn't talk much at the table. I think Mom and Dad didn't want to get into a lot of details about the Fred Sloane thing in front of Robbie.

About 8:00 Aunt Trudy came over and invited Robbie to go out for ice cream with her. As soon as they left, Mom called me into the den where she and Daddy were sitting.

"We thought it would be easier if Robbie weren't around when we do a police report," she told me. "Aunt Trudy offered to help out."

Daddy said, "We're finished trying to talk with Fred Sloane. To think that he would assault you, after all we went through with him yesterday. I'd like to cram my fist down his lying throat."

He paused, looking at Mom. "I know," he said, more calmly. "I'm the one who says violence never works. I sure feel violent right now, though. Let's make that phone call."

13

When Daddy called the sheriff's station they said we could either come in to see them, or they could send a deputy to talk with us at home. Mom wanted to go to the station. I think she didn't want the neighbors to see the black and white squad car in our driveway.

The sheriff's station was only about five miles from our house. On the way over there I felt really nervous. I'd been there once, in the third grade, on a field trip. They showed us their computer, and how they checked to see if someone had a record, or a warrant out for them, and they showed us an empty cell. I thought it was fun then, but I sure didn't feel like this trip was going to be fun.

We walked up to a long counter and waited for someone to notice us. There were three men in the room behind the counter, all in uniforms with badges, and guns in holsters. Two men were sitting at desks, facing us, doing paperwork. The third was leaning against a doorway, talking to someone we couldn't see. When he noticed us he sort of sauntered over to the counter. His uniform was perfectly pressed, with neat creases down each sleeve. He was tall, with dark curly hair and dark skin. He would have been handsome, except he had a big belly hanging over his belt.

"What can I do for you?" he asked, gruffly.

"I'm Les Jenkins. I talked with someone here about half

an hour ago," Daddy said.

"Oh, yes—the child molestation incident, right?"

I felt my stomach twist and knot. I was shocked to hear the words child molestation. It sounded like something terrible that happened to kids I heard about sometimes on the evening news.

Daddy said, "Well, I don't know what to call it, but a neighbor's been after my daughter for months, and I want it stopped."

"Let me get Sergeant Conrad for you. She's in our juvenile division. Have a seat. It'll be a few minutes."

There were two pukey green metal folding chairs against one wall, and two against the other. Mom and I sat down, and Daddy pulled one of the other chairs up beside me. He took hold of my hand and held it gently. You could still see a red spot on my left wrist, where Fred Sloane had grabbed me earlier that day. Nobody said anything. We all sat there like we were most interested in the checkerboard patterns on the floor tiles.

It seemed like we'd been sitting there a long time, but it was really only about ten minutes, when a woman came up to the swinging half-door between the counter and the wall we were sitting against. She held the door open a little.

"Hi. I'm Sergeant Conrad. Would you come back to my office with me?"

We followed her through the door and down a hall to an office in the back of the building. Her office looked really different from the other part of the sheriff's station. I mean, it wasn't like anything you'd see in one of those fancy magazines, but the chairs were soft and comfortable, and her desk was an old wooden one, instead of the metal kind like were in the first big room. And there were plants all over. There was a huge Creeping Charlie plant hanging from the corner of the ceiling near a high window, and there were lots of other little plants on a bookshelf.

Sergeant Conrad sure didn't look like a sergeant. She was tall and skinny—a black woman with really short hair. She was wearing a gray blouse, silk I guess, with a black skirt and black high heels. She looked like she could have been a model.

"Sit down," she said, motioning to the couch. We all three sat together, me in the middle, and she pulled up a chair and sat opposite us. She didn't say anything for a minute, and although she wasn't exactly staring, I had the feeling that she was noticing everything about us. Not just what we were wearing, but how we were sitting, and if our fingernails were clean, and all that stuff.

"Tell me why you're here," she said.

Daddy started. "A man in our neighborhood has been after my daughter for months. I just found out a few days ago. She goes there to babysit, and he won't keep his filthy hands off her."

"And are you here to press charges, Mr. Jenkins?"

"I don't know," Daddy said. "I just want that bastard to know he can't get away with this kind of crap!"

"And you, Mrs. Jenkins? Are you here to press charges?"

Mom sighed. "I don't know what to do," she said.

Sergeant Conrad said, "Why don't you and Mrs. Jenkins go on home? It will take an hour, maybe two, to interview Cassie. Then we'll know more where we stand."

"Maybe we should just wait," Mom said.

"Of course you can wait if you want to. I'll probably want to drive Cassie home anyway, just to get locations straight. I don't drive a black and white, so your neighbors won't notice me," she smiled.

I wondered how she guessed what my mom was worried about, when she didn't even know my mom.

"Well … all right," Mom said. They got up and walked toward the door.

"We'll see you in a little while, Cassie," Daddy said.

I thought he didn't want to leave, but he went out anyway. As the door closed behind them, Sergeant Conrad asked me to tell her all that had happened.

I began again with the same old story. Sergeant Conrad just listened. Even though I'd told the story many times in the past few days, it was still embarrassing and hard to say, and it made me feel dumb and confused. When I'd told as much as I could think of to tell, Sergeant Conrad began asking questions.

"Cassie, do you think this Fred Sloane person does this with other girls, too?"

I told her about Mandy.

"No two people are alike, Cassie, but usually if a man is doing this with one twelve-year-old girl, he'll be doing it with others, too. Most of these guys have a kind of pattern."

I was quiet. I didn't know what else to say. But my stomach wasn't so tight anymore. Sergeant Conrad was pretty easy to talk to.

"I want to tell you some things I've learned on this job, Cassie. Okay?"

"Sure," I said, relieved to have someone else doing the talking for a change.

"Well, first of all, I've learned that these incidents are never the kid's fault. You understand?"

"Never?" I asked. That seemed pretty hard to believe.

"Never, never, never," she said. "Fred Sloane is an adult, and it is his responsibility to act like an adult. That means not exploiting children, no matter what the child has done. Did you ever feel like you were partly to blame for the way Fred was treating you?"

"A little," I admitted. "'Cause, you know, he told me I'd been asking for it, hanging around and all."

"Well, first of all, I don't think you were asking for it. Do you?"

"Not really," I said.

"And second of all, even if you were taking your clothes off and taunting him with sexy belly dances, it would not have been your fault because you are still the child and he is still the adult. Do you see?"

I nodded. I even sort of laughed. The idea of me doing a sexy belly dance was pretty funny.

"Now let me tell you about something else I've learned on this job. Okay?" She was smiling a kind of gentle smile at me. I liked her a lot.

"Girls often feel ashamed, like they've done something dirty, even though the man was forcing himself on them.

Did you ever feel that way?"

I could tell my face was turning red. I looked down at the floor. My throat felt tight. I remembered how I felt when Fred had grabbed me from behind and started rubbing his hands on me and kissing my neck. I didn't say anything.

Sergeant Conrad sat for a while, not saying anything either. Then she told me, "Those feelings are nothing to be ashamed of. All they mean is that your body is working right. Certain things feel good to us. That's how our bodies are made. The Fred Sloanes of the world know that, but they misuse it. You've not done or felt anything to be ashamed of, do you understand, Cassie?"

"I guess."

"It's absolutely wrong for a man of Sloane's age to be getting those feelings from your body. The time for you to be experiencing such things is in a few years, with someone you trust and care about and who is nearer your age. And it's okay for you to start learning these things about your body by yourself, at your own hands, so to speak. But not ever with a guy like Sloane, or with anyone, no matter how old, who is just using you for some kind of thrill. Do you understand, Cassie? You're an innocent victim."

I really didn't want to cry, not in front of Sergeant Conrad. I could feel tears starting anyway, and my nose about to run. She handed me a box of tissues from the top of her desk.

"It's also all right to cry," she smiled at me.

I smiled back, teary eyed. I didn't know why I was crying, except maybe for relief. I was amazed that this Sergeant Conrad, who I'd just met about an hour ago, could know so much about me. She was able to talk to me about my most confusing feelings, and then I didn't feel so confused anymore. What she said made sense to me. I was really glad she'd told me that stuff.

"Let's see, now. Have I missed anything about what I've learned on this job? Maybe I should tell you that a lot of girls your age have similar experiences. Does it help to know that?"

"I guess," I told her. "It really helps to think it wasn't my fault though, or that those other feelings don't mean I'm a dirty person."

"Well, you're not, Cassie. And actually, you're a pretty strong kid. Do you know that?"

I didn't know what to say to that, so I didn't say anything.

"Look, Cassie. You did a lot of the right things. You got help from someone older and you figured out a way to take care of yourself. Now, it didn't all work out exactly as you and Lisa planned, but you were working at it."

"My dad thinks I should have told him and Mom right away," I said.

"Well, yes, that's probably the best thing to do, but if you feel like you can't talk with your parents about something like this, then it's good that you found someone you could talk with. What if this happened to you again, would you be able to tell your parents now?"

"I think so. I feel better with them now than I did a few months ago. I guess now I'd want to tell my parents. Especially my dad."

"What's your biggest worry right now, Cassie?"

I had to think for a while about that one. "I guess I'm still kind of worried about the Sloanes. I mean, I know they'll never like me again and I feel sort of bad about that."

"Because you'll miss Angie, or Fred, or the kids?"

"I guess the kids. Also, I think Angie's feelings are hurt. I don't know, I just have this bad feeling about the Sloanes, even if it's not my fault."

"Well … it will take some time to get past these things. You've been very calm outwardly, through this all. But you've had a lot of inside turmoil, and you've got to keep working at getting it straightened out. I have one more thing to tell you that I've learned on this job, then I'll take you home. Okay?"

"Sure," I said.

"It is very important for every kid who goes through this kind of experience to see a counselor for a while."

"That's what Angie said—that I should see a psychologist," I said. "Do you think there's something wrong with me, too?"

"Not at all. That's back to the false theory that what happened was your fault. That's not the case."

"Then why do I need a counselor if there's nothing wrong with me?"

"You've been caught at a hard time in your own development," Sergeant Conrad said. "You've had to deal with some things which you shouldn't have to deal with yet—kind of like taking a tadpole and expecting it to stay out of water as long as a frog does. Give that tadpole time, and of course it can stay out of water for a long time. But force it to deal with air before it's ready and that's very dangerous for the little ole' tadpole. Are you with me?"

"I guess."

"Now, you're a lot stronger than the tadpole, but you won't get through this experience without a lot of lingering misgivings, unless you see someone who can help you along. What do you think?"

"You don't think I'm sick? Like Angie said?"

"Definitely not."

"She said I couldn't tell the real world from fantasy."

"Well, Angie had her own needs to be met when she said that. Maybe she needed to keep her own fantasy going."

I wondered what she meant by that, but I didn't ask.

"I think you are quite healthy, emotionally. But life will be more fun and less painful for you if you talk through some things with a counselor—just to help you over this rough spot."

"Can't I just come talk to you, Sergeant Conrad?"

"Did I forget to tell you to call me Connie? Sergeant Conrad is such a mouthful, isn't it? Try Connie."

"Can I come and see you instead of some counselor I don't know, Connie?"

I really wanted her to say yes. She knew so much that I didn't know, but she treated me like a grown-up. That was kind of strange, I thought, that she'd been pointing out to me that I was the child, Fred Sloane was the adult, but I felt grownup with her. Maybe like she treated me with respect. Maybe age didn't have anything to do with it.

"You can come see me, Cassie, and you can call me on the phone if you want to talk with me. But I can't be your regular counselor."

"Why not? It's easy for me to talk to you."

"That's good. I like you and I think you're going to

do just fine. But I'm not a trained counselor, and my boss wouldn't like it if I were to do that. Anyway, you need someone who knows different kinds of things than I do."

"I think you know exactly what I need to know," I said.

"Well, I can tell you something more that I know."

"What?" I asked.

"I can tell you the names of some counselors who I know are good."

"Okay," I said, but I still thought the only counselor I wanted was Connie.

"I'll take you home now. I'm certain your parents are anxious."

She picked up her purse, took hold of my arm and led me toward the hallway. "Have we missed anything?" she asked. "Is there anything else you want to talk about?"

"Sort of," I said.

She stopped at the doorway and gave me a searching look.

"If you're a sergeant, why don't you wear a uniform and carry a gun?"

She laughed. "People are more at ease with me if I wear regular clothes. And how do you know I don't carry a gun?"

"Do you?"

She opened her purse and pointed inside. There, tucked into a special holster, was her police revolver.

"Is it loaded?" I asked. I'd never known anyone who carried a gun.

"Of course it's loaded," she said. "I'm a cop! Now come on, let's go."

Once in the car she teased me about how she was one of the original Charlie's Angels, wearing her black disguise. We talked about music. We didn't like the same kind. When we got close to my house, Connie asked me to show her where the Sloanes lived.

As we drove slowly past their house I got that feeling in the pit of my stomach again. It was an empty, lonely feeling. The house had lights on in the den, kitchen and Tina's room. I knew that house as well as my own, and I would never ever go inside it again.

I showed Connie where Fred had stopped me on my way

home from school, and then we drove to my house. Before I got out of the car Connie said, "You know, Cassie, people who behave the way you've told me Fred Sloane behaved are criminals. Certain decisions have to be made about what the next step in this case will be."

It was hard for me to think of Fred as a criminal. Those words, child molester, and criminal, were like icy cold water thrown in my face—they chilled and shocked me.

I saw the curtain pulled to one side and knew my mother must be watching from the living room. We got out of the car and Mom met us at the door. She looked tired, and her eyes were red, like maybe she'd been crying. Daddy brought a cup of coffee in for Connie, and we all sat silently in the living room for what seemed a long time.

"Well?" Daddy said, looking at Connie.

"You folks need to think about whether or not you'll press charges," Connie said.

"I want Cassie to be safe from that scum, that's all I care about," Daddy said. "What would happen if we pressed charges?"

"Would Cassie have to go to court? Testify?" Mom asked.

"Yes, and Lisa, too. Also any eyewitness would be of great help, or any other girls who've had similar experiences with the accused."

I tried to think about what it would be like in court. All I knew about judges and lawyers and courtrooms came from TV. I guessed I would have to tell the whole thing all over again to a lot of people, and in front of Fred. I was feeling all confused again, like I wished I'd never told anyone about Fred Sloane at all. Daddy put his arm around my shoulder and pulled me close to him.

"What would the charges be?" he asked.

"Felony child molestation," Sergeant Conrad answered. "Any touching with sexual intent of a child under fourteen is a felony."

"What if we don't press charges? It's like he's free to do whatever he likes to girls like Cassie. If we do press charges,

Cassie's got to go through the terrible experience of a trial."
Mom looked up from the coffee she'd been sipping.
"Not just Cassie, either. What about Robbie when all of the
neighborhood starts talking? For that matter, Les, what about
us?"

Just like Mom, I thought, to be worrying about Robbie
when I was being put on the spot.

"You're right, Mrs. Jenkins," Connie said. "This kind of
case is hard on the whole family. Cassie seems to be strong,
and her answers to me during the interview were calm and
straightforward. But that interview, difficult as it was, was
nothing like being put on a witness stand. You have to think
about those things."

"So what would you advise, Sergeant Conrad?" Dad asked.
"What if Cassie were your daughter? What would you do?"

"Look, I can't tell you what to do. You've got to make that
decision, as a family."

"Do you think Sloane would be convicted?"

I was getting more and more scared. When my parents
decided to call the cops, I wasn't thinking about any of that
stuff, like trials, and convictions. Would Fred go to prison? I
wondered how things ever got to be so messed up.

"Mr. Jenkins, I can't predict who's going to be convicted
and who isn't. These kinds of questions are more in the realm
of legal advice. Maybe you'll want to talk with a lawyer before
you make a decision about pressing charges."

I looked over at Mom. She was chewing on the edge of
her thumb, her eyebrows pulled together in a deep frown.

"How do we know he won't come after Cassie again?"
Mom asked. "When I first heard of these incidents, I thought
Cassie was in no danger as long as she avoided Fred Sloane.
But after today, when he went out of his way to stop her and
threaten her … " She left the statement hanging.

Connie said, "You don't know what he'll do next. I'll
tell you what I'll do next though, whether you decide to
press charges or not. I'll call him in to the station and set him
straight on some of the basics. If he's worried about his family,
or his reputation, that may be enough to keep him away from
Cassie forever, and other twelve-year-olds for a while. Not for

sure, mind you, but maybe."

"Couldn't we please just forget this? Please?" I asked.

"What do you mean, set him straight on some of the basics?" Mom asked. It was like they hadn't even heard me.

Connie said, "I'll advise him of his rights, then I'll tell him that he's been accused of felony molestation. I'll let him know in very certain terms that he must do everything to avoid being anywhere near Cassie, and that if he sees her, the court could see that as trying to dissuade a potential witness, another serious felony."

"But he'll just say I'm a liar," I told Connie. "And he'll be even madder at me." I could feel my heart pounding and my hands sweating.

"Yes, he probably will say that, Cassie. But he knows the truth, and he's probably going to be worried about people finding out about him. If you've given me an accurate picture of how things have been with him, he's been pretty careful not to be seen, or to get caught by his wife. This says to me that he's a man who wants what he wants, but he doesn't want trouble with it."

"But do you have to call him in? I'm not scared of him. I'll just stay away. I won't even walk anywhere near his house, or the muffler shop. Please?" I was crying again, and wiping my nose on my sleeve. Daddy smoothed my hair and handed me his handkerchief.

"Why are you so worried about Fred being called to the station?" Mom asked.

"I don't know. It just sounds awful to me."

"Cassie," Mom gave me one of her searching looks. "I have to ask you this one more time. Fred Sloane really did all the things you've been telling us about, didn't he? You're not making even a tiny bit of this up, are you?"

"What do you think?" I screamed at her. "Do you think I'm doing this for fun?"

"No, I don't think that at all. But it's a very serious accusation, and you could get us all messed up in a big court case. I just hope you realize how serious this all is," Mom said.

"Really," was all I could say. I was totally disgusted.

Connie turned to me. "Cassie, it's important for all of you

to say what you're feeling, or what you're wondering about, even if it's unpleasant. Don't you think it's better for your mother to ask you that, and to ask for your reassurance, than to keep all those doubts hidden?"

"I guess," I told her, "but I'm not a liar, and she should know that by now."

After we all just sat there, staring at the walls for a while, I got back to my main worry.

"Are you still going to call Fred Sloane into the station tomorrow?"

"Yep," she said. For the first time I thought she was kind of hard, like some of the cops on TV.

"What if he doesn't come?" I asked.

"Then we'll go to his house, or where he works. He'll come, though. He won't want me stopping by just as the family is sitting down to dinner, you know, and talking about child molestation. These guys nearly always come to the station when I call them. Especially the ones with families."

She took three cards from her purse and handed one to each of us. Her name, title, and phone number were on them.

"Please call me if you have any questions, or if you think of anything else I need to know," she said. Then she told my parents some of the same stuff she'd told me in her office, about how important it was for me to see a counselor, and it didn't mean there was anything wrong with me, or them, or any of that. She told them it was often helpful if the whole family went together a few times, and gave us a list of names to choose from.

By the time Connie left it was about 11:30. I went straight to bed. I was trying to think of something happy, watching the shadows on my wall, when Daddy came in and sat on the edge of the bed.

"It's going to be all right," he told me, resting his hand on my shoulder. "Try not to worry."

He bent his face to mine, kissed me on the cheek, and walked quietly out of my room.

I did try not to worry, but it didn't work. All I could think of were words like child molestation and criminal and felony and court and all of the pictures that went with them. And I felt sorry for Fred, and scared, and I felt terrible knowing that Connie was going to see him the next day.

I was mad at my mom again, too. And all of that stuff Connie had told me about not feeling guilty, or ashamed, wasn't making as much sense as it had when she was talking to me. I was all mixed up again, and I didn't like it. I made myself think about being at the beach with Grammy, and I finally fell asleep.

14

My mother woke me earlier than usual. "Get up, Cassie, I want you to be ready in time for me to drop you off at school."

I groaned. I hated having to wake up in the morning. Mom did her usual open-the-curtains routine, and I did my usual pull-the-pillow-over-my-head routine. The sun was already bright and warm coming in through my window.

"It's going to be hot today. Come on, Cassie." She shook my shoulder, then took the pillow from my head. "I'm going to drive you to and from school for a while, until things calm down. I don't want you to be faced with Fred Sloane again."

I dragged myself out of bed and into the shower. Fred Sloane, Fred Sloane, Fred Sloane, I thought. It's the last thing I hear at night and the first thing I hear in the morning. I turned the water on full blast, hot, and stepped in. I stayed for a long time, feeling the sting of the water on my body, and worrying about what was going to happen when Connie called him to the station.

At school, before first period, Mandy came to get my geography homework.

"Sorry," I told her. "I didn't do any homework last night."

"But, Cassie, I depend on you," she whined. "You've let me down, Old Buddy."

I looked into her clear blue eyes and her lightly freckled face.

"Maybe you ought to start doing it yourself," I told her. "Or better yet, maybe I could depend on you for a change."

She looked shocked. "Well excuse me," she said sarcastically, and walked on to class without looking back.

I followed, way behind her. Everybody said hi to Mandy as they walked past her, even the eighth graders. Hardly anyone even noticed me. I felt awful. Even though Mandy could have been best friends with almost anyone, she was always my best friend, and now I'd been mean and stupid.

Valerie Biggers was absent from Marlow's class, so I had to sit up front in my assigned seat, instead of in front of Mandy. I felt lonely, and I was bored with prepositional phrases. I wrote a note to Mandy. I wrote "Y-R-R-O-S" in great big letters on a piece of notebook paper, folded it about ten times, wrote her name on the front and passed it to Danny, behind me.

In the fifth grade we always used to write backwards notes to each other. We thought it was a secret code. In a few minutes Danny tapped me on the shoulder and handed the note back to me. Written in teeny tiny letters under my big ones was "o-o-t e-m."

At lunchtime we sat on the front steps again. Mandy was sure Eric would be there.

"I just want to see him," she told me. "I like to look at Eric. Don't you like to look at Jason?"

"I don't know. I never thought about it." It seemed kind of funny, wanting to look at someone like that.

"Don't you think about Jason a lot? I think about Eric all the time."

"I guess I don't," I told her. "I kind of like him, but maybe not as much as you like Eric."

"I think I'm in love," she told me.

"I don't think I'll ever be in love," I told Mandy.

"Not ever in love!" she screeched. "Why not? That's stupid. You're just saying that because you don't know. Why wouldn't you ever fall in love?"

"It's too confusing," I told her. "And if you fall in love, then sooner or later you've got to have sex, and that's really confusing."

"Well, yeah. I guess. But people seem to like it," she told me.

"Don't you think you will?"

"I'm not sure," I said. And then I told her all about Sergeant Conrad, and the stuff we talked about. "It helped to talk with her, but I still feel all confused."

"So confused you can't even do your geography homework," Mandy said, giving me that innocent smile. "I'll help. I'll do geography tonight, and you can copy it in the morning."

"Thanks a lot. You're probably even willing to do our geography assignments every Tuesday night, Tuesday being the one day of the week we don't get geography homework."

"Sure. I can do that," she smiled, then froze. "Look, it's Eric," she sighed. "Isn't he beautiful?"

I swear, I thought I was going to throw up. "Beautiful isn't exactly what I'd call Eric," I said.

"That's 'cause you don't know about love," she whispered. Eric was way over on the other side of the steps, not even looking in our direction, but she whispered anyway.

I knew she was kidding. But it was true. I didn't know about love. I didn't even know about like.

I wanted to tell Mandy how scared I was about Fred being called in to the sheriff's station, but Mom had said not to talk about Fred at all, even to Mandy. I probably would have told her anyway, except she was so busy looking at Eric I was afraid she might not hear me.

Mom was waiting for me when school was over, just like she said she'd be. Robbie was in the backseat, pressing his nose flat against the side window and sticking his tongue out at me. He was getting the window all yucky. Mom had made special arrangements to get off from work early for a week or so. I guess she really was worried about me.

We stopped for ice cream on the way home. I got my favorite, a double dip chocolate chip on a sugar cone. Mom just got sherbet because she was watching her weight. Robbie got a chocolate sundae, no nuts. I'd only had about two bites of my ice cream when I dropped the whole thing on the floor. It wasn't important, but I felt like crying. Robbie handed me his sundae.

"You can have mine, Cassie," he said, smiling. "I'm not so hungry."

That did it. I started to cry. Sometimes I can't stand for people to be too nice to me.

"It's okay, Cassie," he said. "Eat some." So I did. I stopped crying almost as soon as I'd started, but I felt funny about it.

In the car Mom said to me, "I know this has been hard on you. I think Sergeant Conrad is right about counseling. Let's call one of those numbers when we get home."

I nodded. It really didn't matter much to me whether we called or not. All I wanted was to be at the beach with Grammy, and then to come back in September and have the whole Fred Sloane thing be gone.

When we drove into our driveway, Angie was parked in front waiting for us. She got out of the car, yelling at Tina and Dorian to stay in the backseat. She walked over to where I was getting out of the car and started screaming at me.

"You liar! You're coming with me right now down to the sheriff and you're going to tell her what a liar you are!"

She was shaking me by the shoulders and screaming in my face. She looked wild! Mom ran over to us and tried to pull Angie's hands away from me.

"Angie! Stop! This won't help!" she said.

Angie just kept screaming at the top of her lungs, "Liar! Liar! Liar!"

"I'm no liar!" I yelled back. "I don't lie! Leave me alone!" I tried to get away from her but she was hanging on tight. I kicked and shoved, but still she hung on. Mom was yelling at her to stop all the time we were yelling at each other. I could hear kids crying and the dog across the street barking. Angie reached for my hair and started pulling. It hurt like anything.

"STOP! ANGIE! STOP!" Mom yelled. She yanked at Angie's arm one more time and when Angie didn't let loose, she turned and ran to the garden hose. My head was hurting and Angie kept pulling and screaming.

"Liar! You're no different than the others! Trying to hurt my Fred!"

Then I felt water splashing on me. Mom had the hose aimed right at Angie's face, turned on full blast. Angie spit and sputtered and then let go. She turned away from the blast of water, but Mom kept it coming. She ran to her car and Mom ran after her, still spraying her.

"Get out of here and stay out!" Mom screamed. "You leave Cassie alone! Both of you!"

Angie opened the door to get in the car and Mom sprayed water straight inside. She kept aiming the spray at the car, even after it was out of range. My head hurt and my face was scratched. Robbie was crying and old Mr. Putnam had come outside and was staring at us with his mouth open. I was soaking wet. Mom was crying, still holding the blasting hose.

"Robbie, turn the water off, please," Mom sobbed, dropping the hose. She came over to me and hugged me and we both cried and cried. Robbie was hugging our legs and pulling at my hand.

"Why was Angie hurting you, Cassie?" he asked. Mr. Putnam walked over to where we were standing. "Are you all right?" he asked.

I nodded.

"What was that all about anyway?" he wanted to know. "I bought this house to retire in because it was such a quiet neighborhood." He was looking at my mother out of his cloudy blue-gray eyes. He was a little man, kind of shriveled looking.

"Don't worry, Mr. Putnam," Mom told him. "I don't think this will happen again."

He smiled a feeble smile. "You sure took care of that woman, didn't you, Mrs. Jenkins?"

"I sure did," Mom said.

"Just like a mother hen, protecting her chick," Mr. Putnam laughed. "My, but that was a sight to see."

He seemed to be enjoying the whole thing now. I could see he was ready to talk on and on. I guess Mom saw that coming, too. She said, "Thank you for your concern, Mr.

Putnam, but I think I'd better get Cassie inside and into some dry clothes."

"Yes, you'd better, Mother Hen," he giggled, then shuffled back to his own yard.

We walked inside, Mom still with her arm around me and Robbie holding my hand. Mom sat me on a bar stool under the light in the kitchen and checked my face and neck for scratches. There was only one scratch and several little red spots. My shoulders hurt a little where Angie had held me so tightly, but I wasn't hurt much. Mom took a cotton ball soaked in alcohol and cleaned the scratch.

"If there's as much poison in Angie's fingernails as there is in her heart, we've got to be very careful not to let this scratch get infected," Mom said.

Robbie crawled up onto the stool next to mine.

"Why, Cassie? Why was Angie hurting you?"

Once Robbie asked a question, he didn't forget about it until it got answered.

"She's mad at me," I told him.

"Yeah, but why? Why did she say bad things about you, like you're a liar and everything?"

"It's complicated," Mom told Robbie. "You'll just have to understand that she was very angry. It was not at all Cassie's fault, and Cassie's not a liar, and that's enough for you to know right now." She was looking me over again.

"Are you sure you're all right, Cassie? I thought she was angry enough to kill you. It scared me." She put her arms around me again.

"It scared me, too. It was awful. It was like Angie was a total stranger. And she was so strong, I couldn't even begin to get loose. You were great, Mom. I've never seen you do anything like that before. As soon as you started with the hose, I knew I'd be safe," I smiled.

I thought I could feel Mom crying again. Her body was shaking and she was sort of gasping for air. But when I pulled back to look at her, she wasn't crying at all. She was laughing.

"I didn't know what else to do," she gasped through

her laughter. "It sure worked, though. I wish your dad had been here to see my heroic hose act."

She laughed and flexed her muscles. I was laughing, too. Just the thought of my sensible mother chasing someone around with a garden hose, blasting water … It was pretty funny.

Robbie began shrieking, the way he does when he's all excited about a story he's telling. "Her hair was hanging down, and dripping wet, and Mom's face looked like a bulldog!" We all laughed even harder.

Robbie said, "Boy, I bet Tina and Dorian know who's boss now!"

The thought of Tina and Dorian stopped my laughter. It was a relief to think of Angie as a madwoman or a villain or something. But Tina and Dorian? In the back of my mind I thought I could hear them crying when Angie was yelling at me.

Mom sighed. "Tina and Dorian."

We were quiet for a while.

"What a mess," Mom said.

She put her arms around me again and kissed me on top of the head like she used to when I was little.

"I love you," she told me. "I thought about what Sergeant Conrad said last night. I know you're not a liar, and I think we did the right thing by talking with her. I'm nervous about this thing, too—you know, like what will the neighbors think, and if some of the boys at school hear about it, will it ruin your reputation. I'm sorry I'm not more on top of things for you, Cassie, like your father is."

I pushed away from her a little, so I could see her face. She looked worried.

"You were on top of things today, when you got the hose out," I said.

We both laughed again. I liked her better that day than I had for a long, long time. It's hard to stay critical of a person who's just saved your life with a garden hose.

I changed clothes, and then Mom and Robbie and I went down to KFC. We got home just as Daddy was driving into the driveway. Mom and I made a salad, and we put out paper plates.

"I wasn't expecting a picnic," Daddy said, kind of sarcastically. He doesn't like to eat from paper plates.

"Well, some things happened here today that we weren't expecting, either," Mom said, and then went on to tell him the story.

"What do you think Angie meant when she told Cassie she was no different than the others?" Daddy asked.

"I have no idea, Les. Even at the time, in the middle of all that water, I thought it sounded strange. What do you think, Cassie?"

"I don't know."

"Maybe this has happened with Fred before," Daddy said. I wondered if all of this Fred Sloane business was ever going to stop.

I went to bed kind of early that night, and I took my vocabulary cards with me. I'd heard that if you studied something just before sleep, it stayed in your brain better. I was propped up against my pillows, going through my cards, when Robbie came in wearing pajamas and smelling of toothpaste. I think Robbie eats toothpaste instead of brushing his teeth with it.

"Dorian's not my friend anymore," he told me, climbing into bed beside me.

"You mean because of what happened today, with Angie?"

"Yeah. And stuff."

"What stuff?" I asked.

"At school today he said you were a bad girl."

"And what did you say?"

"I said shut up, and you're not my friend, but then I didn't have anybody to play with at recess time."

"Couldn't you play with someone else?" I asked.

"But no one I like as much as Dorian. Dorian's my best, most fun friend. I mean, he was, before."

Robbie was frowning, and picking at the lint from my blanket. I thought of Dorian, how serious he would be when we were playing games, and then he'd just start laughing hysterically, like Robbie does. And I thought of all the forts they'd made, with towels and boxes, and how the two of them would play together for hours.

"Maybe it will be okay," I told him.

He kept at the lint.

"Maybe," he said, but I could see he wasn't convinced. I wasn't convinced either.

"Is it okay if I sleep with you tonight?" he asked me.

"Sure," I said.

He always kicks a lot in his sleep, and my bed's not very big, so usually I won't let him sleep with me. But I felt kind of sorry for him that night, and I felt close to him, too. Even if he was real young, and kind of spoiled, he was my friend and I was his.

I kept thinking and rethinking the fight in my mind. Angie hated me. That was obvious. But I wondered again what she'd meant when she said I was no different from the others. The fight had been awful, but in a way it was exciting. It was exhilarating—exhilarating was one of my vocabulary words.

I was still real worried about stuff. Daddy had called Sergeant Conrad to tell her about the fight and ask her to put a restraining order on both Fred and Angie. And I felt very sad about Dorian and Tina. Things were in a terrible mess. Still, I felt better than I had a few days ago. Maybe I was getting used to having things in a mess. Or maybe it helped, knowing that Mom cared enough about me to fight for me.

Robbie kicked me in the stomach and I moved over to the other side of the bed. I put my left leg over both of his legs, just to hold them down. The shadows on the wall were playing soccer.

15

Mandy caught up to me just before first period. "Did Jason call you last night?"

"No, why?"

"Eric called me last night. He and Jason want us to meet them at the Cineplex Friday night."

"Nobody called me," I said. "I don't think Jason even likes me anymore."

"But he does. Eric told me that Jason likes you a lot. He's just shy. Hey, Cassie!"

Mandy grabbed my hand like she'd just had a brilliant idea.

"Let's look in your locker! I'll bet there's a note from Mr. Shy Guy."

The warning bell rang.

"After class," I told her.

I thought Mandy was more excited about me and Jason than I was. She was right though. In my locker was a big picture of this really ugly looking cartoon guy. It was a character Jason drew a lot. He, the character that is, had this big, crooked nose with a wart on the end of it. His head was real big and his body was about the total same size as his head.

He was wearing heavy-looking boots, with chains wrapped around his neck, arms, and legs. Under the picture it said, "Don't be a punk. Tell Jason you'll meet him at the

Cineplex Friday night."

It made me laugh. I folded the picture carefully and put it in a special section in my notebook.

At lunchtime, Mandy and Julia and I went out to the front steps. Julia and Mandy talked about boys and love, and I listened and wished I had more to say. I couldn't take my eyes off Mandy's Twinkie. She finally got the hint and offered it to me, but she'd already eaten more than half of it.

Eric and Jason came over just as I had stuffed the last of the Twinkie into my mouth. I was embarrassed. My mouth was so full I couldn't even open it to say hi. Eric talked with Mandy and Julia while Jason stood looking at his feet, and I sat trying to swallow the Twinkie. Jason and I didn't even look at each other until Eric said "Later," and turned to walk away. Then Jason moved closer to me and tapped me on the shoulder. I looked up.

"Say yes, Cassie," he whispered.

"Yes," I whispered back.

He smiled this really big smile and then ran to catch up with Eric. His smile did kind of knock me out. He wasn't much on conversation, but he sure had a great smile, braces and all.

"Nice smile," I said to Mandy and Julia. That cracked them up. I didn't mean it to be funny, but they both fell apart laughing.

"You like him, all right, Miss Cool," Mandy said, still laughing. "Look at you, all cow eyes over a metal mouth smile."

That got Julia laughing even harder. She tried not to spit out her soda and gave this little choke and blew her nose instead. That was so gross I started laughing so hard I almost wet my pants. Talk about gross! I ran into the girl's room, Mandy and Julia chasing after me, laughing even harder. I made it just in time.

They were splashing water on their faces, getting control of themselves, when I came out of the stall. Mandy splashed water on my face and I suddenly pictured the whole water hose thing of the day before, which started me laughing all over again. I don't know why—it just seemed so funny. I was so weak I had to lean against the sink to keep from falling over. Finally though, when the eighth graders started coming in to put on their lipstick before class, we managed to get calm enough to walk to fifth period.

When Mom and Robbie got me from school that day, Mom told me that Daddy had talked with a lawyer, and with Sergeant Conrad again, and that she had made an appointment for me with one of the counselors.

"I'm kind of scared to see a counselor," I told her.

"She, Betty Shipper is her name, said she'd like to see the three of us together for the first time. Will that be easier?" Mom asked.

"Maybe."

"Let's just give it a try, Cassie. If it's awful, we'll stop."

"Okay," I said.

We stopped by Lisa's house on the way home so Mom could return a big roasting pan she'd borrowed. Aunt Trudy and Lisa were both home. Sometimes Aunt Trudy works weekends and is home during the week.

Lisa fixed lemonade for us all, and we sat outside. Aunt Trudy was wearing a T-shirt that said "A woman without a man is like a fish without a bicycle," and purple cut-off sweatpants with red high top Keds. She was wearing a white terry cloth headband, with wings on each side.

"What's new in the Jenkins/Sloane department?" Aunt Trudy asked.

"What a mess this has all been," Mom said. Then she told about Fred stopping me on the way home from school, and the water fight with Angie, and the restraining order.

"Weren't you scared when Fred stopped you?" Lisa asked me.

"I was really more scared with Angie," I told her. "It was like Angie was a crazy woman!"

"Wow, what a trip! Aren't you scared she'll try to get you again?" Lisa asked.

"I hadn't even thought about that. Thanks a lot for bringing it up," I said, sarcastically.

"If either Angie or Fred gets anywhere near Cassie we can have them arrested," Mom said. "It seems as if when Sergeant Conrad called Fred into the station, that set Angie off. But now Connie has talked with Angie, too—told her that assault is a serious crime, and so is any kind of intimidation of a potential witness."

"Do you think that's the end of it then?" Aunt Trudy asked.

"Who knows? I asked Sergeant Conrad the same thing. She said she wouldn't make any guesses, and that she couldn't tell me anything about how either Fred or Angie responded when they were at the station. She said it would be an invasion of their privacy."

Aunt Trudy groaned. "They sure weren't worried about invading Cassie's privacy, either of them! Sometimes the law burns me up!"

"Trudy," Mom said, in her sisterly, pleading voice.

"Well, it does, Helen! Doesn't that anger you? I mean, really."

"Well, yes, in a way it does. But I do respect this Sergeant Conrad. She's been very helpful to us."

"So are you just going to drop it, or have Fred arrested, or what?"

"We'll talk more about that after Les gets home this evening. A lot of what happens is up to Cassie. You know, whether or not she wants to go through the hassle of being the main witness against him. Lisa would probably have to testify, too."

My stomach was doing its thing again—tightening and churning at words like arrest and testify.

"Oh, no," Lisa moaned. "What if I don't want to testify?"

"You probably wouldn't have any choice," Aunt Trudy said. "They'd subpoena you if they thought you'd be an important witness."

"Yes, and Mandy, too," Mom said.

"Mandy?" Lisa said. "Why Mandy?"

"I think Fred tried something with her once, too," Mom explained. "Isn't that what she told you, Cassie?"

"Yeah, just that he brushed his hand across her ... chest."

"I've been talking with one of the psychologists at the hospital," Aunt Trudy said. "These Fred Sloane types usually follow a pattern, according to Dr. Sturm. I didn't talk with her about Cassie, specifically, but I told her I'd heard of a case, and what did she know about men who do that kind of thing—were they likely to get violent, or commit rape, or incest with their own kids—that kind of thing."

"So what did this doctor tell you?" Mom asked.

"Well, she told me that these guys usually stay with a particular age, or time of development. For instance, Fred Sloane is probably mainly interested in girls who are just beginning to develop. When Cassie starts to look more grown-up, be more fully developed, he'd probably stop trying to fool around with her."

"What about rape, or some other violent stuff?" I asked, feeling scared again.

"Dr. Sturm says you can't really depend on anything with men like this. They're usually not killers. Some of them rape, but most of them just want to fondle the girl, sexually, and maybe take off her clothes—maybe take off his clothes, too, or at least expose his penis to her. Did Fred ever do that, expose himself to you?" she asked me.

"No!"

I was shocked by the idea of that. I wondered if he would have done that, if Angie hadn't come home early the last time I babysat. How gross!

"She also said that a lot of them, if they're married, or have jobs, are pretty careful not to get caught. So if they're confronted, by a parent, or by the police, even though they deny everything and show a lot of bravado, they're very frightened about being found out, and they'll control themselves for a while, out of fear."

"Why would a grown-up man be like that anyway?" Lisa asked.

"Who knows. Dr. Sturm said there are a lot of theories, but the one that makes the most sense to her has to do with the man feeling very inadequate, and being unable to have a satisfying relationship with an adult."

"Angie and Fred seemed happy together," I said. Mom

and Lisa both nodded in agreement.

"Yes, but you can never tell, can you, what goes on behind closed doors. It may just have been an act. Dr. Sturm said that sometimes a man will marry someone who also has a lot of hang-ups about sex, but who wants the illusion of a happy marriage. Then they can live in a kind of make-believe world. No pressure on her for sex and no pressure on him to perform for her."

I was having a hard time thinking about that stuff. It sounded to me like sex was more trouble than it was worth, except maybe for having kids.

Robbie came out from where he'd been watching TV. "Can we go home now, Mom? I don't like their TV." Aunt Trudy grabbed Robbie and held him on her lap, tickling him.

"So, thanks a lot, Mr. Slob. What's so terrible about my TV, huh?"

Robbie was squirming around, trying to get loose, and laughing. "Too small, Aunt Trudy Cootie," he managed to gasp.

"Get out of here, Mr. Rob Glob," she said, putting him down on the grass next to her and tousling his hair.

"It really is getting close to dinnertime. I didn't mean to stay so long," Mom said.

Lisa walked out to the car with us.

"I can hardly wait for summer," she told me. "Three more weeks and it's all over until September."

"I can't wait to go to Grammy's," I told her. "Are you going to come stay with us, too?"

"I want to," she said. "I think I may get a part-time job at the bank though, and I want to do that, too. At least I could come down on weekends still."

"What would Ray Gun say if you were gone on the weekends?" Aunt Trudy teased.

"Mommm," Lisa whined. "I hate it when you call Raymond by that stupid Ray Gun name."

"He thinks I'm cute though, doesn't he?" Aunt Trudy gave me an exaggerated wink. "Huh, Lisa?" Lisa rolled her eyes.

"He only said that once, and I'm sorry I ever told you. It was probably before he knew you very well, anyway," Lisa said. We all laughed.

On the way home Mom said, "It was a relief to me to hear that most men like Fred Sloane back off once they've been confronted by the police. I know nothing's certain, but I hope he follows the pattern."

"What pattern?" Robbie asked from the back.

"Oops," Mom said. "I forgot about the little person in the backseat." She smiled. I smiled back. I kind of liked it that Mom had forgotten about Robbie. Usually I thought she forgot about me when Robbie was around, instead of forgetting about Robbie when I was around.

"What pattern?" Robbie insisted.

"It's too grown-up for you, Robbie. Just forget about it," Mom told him. For once he did.

Later that evening Mom and Daddy and I talked about what to do next. We told Daddy what Aunt Trudy had said, and Daddy told us about what the lawyer had said. We talked for a long time. The lawyer had said a lot depended upon the judge or jury if we pressed charges. It would be harder to get a conviction without any eyewitnesses, but Mandy's testimony would back me up as far as showing a pattern. Mostly it would hinge on me, if I could keep my story straight, and not be confused by some badgering defense lawyer. There was no certainty of how things would turn out. Even if he was convicted, he could end up with a suspended sentence of some kind of mandatory counseling.

"It's a dilemma," Daddy said. "I don't want to put Cassie through a traumatic trial, and I don't want Fred Sloane just to go free and keep doing the same routine on twelve-year-olds. I don't know. What do you think, Cassie?"

"I think I just want to go to Grammy's in three weeks, and forget everything else," I said.

"I don't want her to testify," Mom said. "Maybe it's selfish of me, but we've had enough agony over this whole thing as it is."

"But what's right?" Daddy said. "Is it right just to drop it and do nothing?"

"I don't know, Les. I love you for always wondering what's right. But what if we go through all that misery, and he's not even convicted?"

"Yes, but what about him? What if he keeps preying on innocent young girls?" Daddy said

We went back and forth and round and round, saying the same things for a long time.

16

Friday night at the movies with Jason and Eric and Mandy was great. A lot of other kids we knew from school were there, too. When the movie was over we went out the back way. It was real dark in the short walkway. Eric and Mandy were walking ahead of us. Jason and I were holding hands.

Before we reached the back door, Jason pulled me to the side and kissed me. It was more that we just touched lips, really, than it was a kiss. I sort of hugged him, and then we went out the door into the parking lot and caught up with Eric and Mandy. It was nothing like having Fred Sloane's mouth on mine. It was gentle, and shy, and I liked it. I liked Jason. I thought about him a lot the rest of the weekend—his eyes, his smile, but mostly his kiss. Maybe I could fall in love someday after all.

Monday my English term paper was due. I finished it in a hurry Sunday night. Jack London was my subject, and I'd started out being interested, going to the library and taking notes and all of that stuff you're supposed to do. But I ended up doing a sloppy job.

Wednesday afternoon was our first appointment with Dr. Shipper. I called Connie when I got home.

"Is Sergeant Conrad there?" I asked.

When Connie picked up the phone she said, "Cassie, I'm glad you called. I've been wondering about you."

"I decided I don't want to go to court," I told her. "Are you mad at me?"

"Of course not," she told me. "That's your decision, not mine. How's life treating you these days?"

"Okay, I guess. I don't think I'll get a very good report card this time."

"Well, you've had a lot of other things on your mind. You can make up for it in September. What about the Sloanes? Have you seen any of them since the restraining order was issued last week?"

"No."

"Good," she said. "How's the counseling going?"

"I don't like it," I told her.

"How many times have you been?"

"Just once," I answered.

"Cassie, will you promise me that you'll see the counselor at least four times?"

"But I don't like her very much. Besides, what good does it do just to talk?"

"Plenty," Connie said. "Give it a fair try, will you?"

I did a quick calculation. It was Wednesday, June 3. School would be out on the twelfth, and I was going to Grammy's the following Monday.

"That means I'd have to see her three more times. I don't know if I'll have time for that or not," I said.

"Make time," Connie told me. "And make one more appointment for when you get back in September. Then quit if it's no good. But at least try it."

"Okay," I said. "I will."

"If I don't see you before you go to your grandmother's, have a good time, will you?"

"It'll be great. I'm going to swim all day and eat pizza all night," I said, remembering what Grammy had told me.

"Send me a postcard," she said. "Or better yet, send me a pizza—mushrooms and pepperoni."

I had to see Dr. Shipper again the next Wednesday. The first time I went in with Mom and Daddy, but this time I went in by myself.

We talked about some of the same things I had talked with Connie about at the sheriff's station. But it wasn't as easy for me to talk with Dr. Shipper. Maybe because she was older, and she wore big, thick glasses that made her eyes look all funny.

"Cassie, how do you feel about coming here?" she asked me, after a long silence in our conversation.

"I'm really just doing it because Connie wants me to," I told her.

"Well, that's an honest answer. What do you want to do?" she asked.

"I don't know," I said.

"Do you usually know what you want to do?" she asked.

"I don't know," I said. Boy, was I sounding dumb.

"How do you decide what you're going to do, say, on a Friday night?"

"Well, sometimes someone asks me to do something. Like last Friday night I went to the movies with some friends."

"What if no one asks you to do anything. Then what?"

"Well, then sometimes I do something with my family, or read, or watch TV."

"Do you ever decide you want to do something, like see a special movie, or go someplace special, or play tennis, anything, and then get someone to do that with you?"

I didn't say anything. I'd only been there about ten minutes and already I was tired of her questions.

She waited. When I still didn't answer, she said, "In other words, do you ever make plans yourself? Or do you wait for others to make plans for you?"

That was a hard question, and I didn't see what it had to do with anything.

"I guess someone else usually makes the plans," I said.

"Is there something you want to do this weekend? Something you can arrange?"

"I don't know," I said. Was this ever boring! All I could think of to say was I don't know.

"All right, Cassie. I'm going to give you an assignment. Figure out, for yourself, one thing you want to do this weekend. Then you make it happen."

"Like what?" I said.

"Anything. It doesn't have to be a big deal. It can be something as small as meeting a friend at the mall. It doesn't even have to include anyone else. Maybe it could be going jogging by yourself. The important thing is that you decide, and that you do it. Understand?"

"I guess," I said. "But I don't see what this has to do with the stuff with Fred Sloane."

"A lot of what we'll talk about together won't be directly related to your experiences with Mr. Sloane," Dr. Shipper said. "But everything is one way or another related to everything else, so we'll just follow where our conversations naturally take us."

She lost me with that statement, but I nodded my head anyway.

"The reason for this assignment is that it is important for you to get to know what's right for you—not because Sergeant Conrad thinks it's right, or your parents think it's right, but because you think it's right. That's part of growing up, learning your mind."

I'd never really thought of it that way. My parents, and teachers, too, seemed to think growing up had to do with getting me to act the way they did. I liked Dr. Shipper's ideas of growing up better.

"I still don't see what any of this has to do with Fred Sloane," I said.

"Learning your own mind has a lot to do with Fred Sloane," she said. "What would you do if you were starting all over again, that first night when Mr. Sloane became aggressive with you? How would you handle that now?"

I thought about it for a while. "Well, I know for sure I would never babysit there again, after the first time."

"Would you do anything else differently?"

"If my mom tried to get me to babysit over there, I'd just tell her that I didn't like the way Fred Sloane was acting, and I wouldn't go over there anymore."

"Would that have been easier in the long run than the way it really happened?"

I laughed. "Lots," I said.

She smiled. "The reason you would do that differently if it happened again is that you know more about yourself now than you did then. You were very confused when all of this started. You had a right to be confused. Any twelve-year-old would be."

I nodded.

"So getting to know more about yourself, what's right for you, does relate to your experiences with Fred Sloane. Do you see?"

I nodded again. I really did see what she was getting at, sort of.

Her desk timer went off, which meant my hour was up. She handed me an assignment reminder on a three by five card. It said, "You arrange it—one thing you want to do."

"See you next week," she said.

"Bye, Dr. Shipper," I said, and walked out to where Mom was waiting.

I wondered a lot about that assignment. I honestly didn't know what I wanted to do.

I still didn't have any ideas on Saturday when I ran down to the market to get some milk for lunch. There were two kids out front. They had a big box with six kittens in it.

"Want a kitten?" the girl asked me. She was about eight years old.

"I do want a kitten," I said. "But my mom won't let us have pets."

"Is your mom mean?" the little girl asked.

"No. She just thinks animals are dirty," I explained.

"Not cats," the little girl said.

All this time I was looking in the box, watching the kittens. There were four gray ones and two orange and white ones. I wanted the orange one who kept climbing on top of the others, trying to get out of the box.

I looked at cat food and kitty litter on my way to pick up the milk. I looked at the kittens one more time on my way out. I thought about my assignment, to do something I wanted. I really wanted that little orange kitten.

"Will you save this orange one for me, for an hour?" I asked.

"Okay," the girl said. "When will an hour be?"

"Just save it until I come back," I told her. "Even if I can't get it, I'll come back and tell you."

"Okay," she said.

"Be sure not to give it to anyone else," I insisted.

"I won't," she promised.

On the way home I tried to figure out the best way to convince Mom that I should get the kitten. Daddy would be easy. But Mom ... ?

"Mom, I saw the cutest little kitten at the market today," I said at lunch. "It was orange and white and so playful." Mom didn't say anything.

"Cats are clean, Mom, and I'd take care of it."

"Oh, Cassandra, please," Mom said. "You know how I feel about pets."

Robbie started whining. "You never let us have pets. Everyone else gets animals, but not us. You're not a nice mommy." He was getting carried away.

"What if we just tried it for a week?" I asked. "Then if I didn't take care of it, or if it was too dirty, we could take it back."

"They wouldn't do that, Cassie. They're trying to get rid of those cats."

"But what if they would, Mom? What if they would?"

"I don't know," she said.

I felt like jumping up and down and clapping my hands. "I don't know" was the closest thing to yes she'd ever said when it came to getting a cat or a dog. But I stayed cool.

"I'd help," Robbie said. "I'd even go to bed on time every night if you'd let us get a kitty. Please, Mom. You really are a nice mommy. Please?" he begged.

"What about when you kids go to Santa Monica? Then I'll be stuck taking care of a kitten," Mom said.

"We'll take it with us. I'll call Grammy right now."

I ran out of the room before Mom had a chance to say no. Grammy agreed. She said she thought it would be fun.

"Just bring a litter box and a box with a towel or something in it so it will have a warm place to sleep."

"Thanks, Grammy. Thanks, thanks, thanks!" I said, and hung up. I didn't even think to say good-bye.

"Grammy says it's okay with her," I yelled at Mom from the hallway.

"I'll go get the kitten right now. Okay? Want to come, Robbie? Okay, Mom?"

Mom sighed. "Oh, okay. I'll hate myself in the morning, but I guess it's okay to try. But the minute you don't feed it or clean up after it, it's good-bye cat. Do you understand?"

"For sure," I said, as Robbie and I ran out the door to pick up the kitten.

She was soooo cute. Robbie and I made a place for her to sleep in my bathroom. We put a kitty litter box in there, and some water. We put some tuna-flavored cat food in a saucer and piled some old towels in a corner so she'd have a soft warm place to sleep. Mostly though, we held her and watched her. We got a long piece of string and teased her with it. She ended up getting all tangled up in it, so we named her Tangle.

Mom was in there watching when Tangle knocked over my bathroom wastebasket and crawled inside. She was buried in tissues, with only her fluffy orange tail showing, twitching. Mom laughed so hard, I knew we'd never have to take Tangle back.

Early in the morning Robbie came into my room to check on the kitten. She'd slept all night on the towels in my bathroom, and she even used the litter box, like she was supposed to do. Robbie picked her up and put her on my bed, then he climbed in. She walked on my pillow and started chewing my hair.

"Maybe Dorian would like to see me again if I called him and told him he could see Tangle," Robbie said.

"You'd better only see Dorian at school," I told Robbie.

"Yeah, but he's never going to play with me again!" Robbie said, getting louder with each word. "And he'd like Tangle, so then he'd like me. I'm going to call him right now," he said, climbing out of my bed.

I grabbed his arm.

"That's not a good idea," I told him.

"Yes, it is! Dorian loves kitties!"

"Yes, but Dorian can't come over anymore," I told him.

"Why not? Why not?"

"Because!" I yelled at him. "The Sloanes hate me and I hate them and none of us can ever even see each other again!"

"I'm going to call anyway!" he yelled. "You're not my boss! You're not my boss! YOU'RE NOT MY BOSS!"

He went running to the hall phone, picked it up, and started dialing. I ran after him, grabbed the receiver from him and slammed it back. Daddy came out of their bedroom, rubbing his eyes.

"What's all this commotion about so early on a Sunday morning?" he asked.

"Cassie's bossing me around and I want to call Dorian," Robbie said.

"Cassie's right, Robbie, you can't call Dorian."

Daddy reminded Robbie of how Angie had treated me, and said that Fred had treated me even worse, and that we were never to go to the Sloanes' house again, and that none of the Sloanes were ever to come to our house.

"Try to be friends with Dorian at school," Daddy said. "It's not Dorian's fault his parents are like that. But school's the only place you can see him ... Come on now, help me fix pancakes."

I went back to my room to check on Tangle. I felt sorry for Robbie, but I felt great about how I'd completed my counseling assignment. In fact, I could hardly wait for the next session with Dr. Shipper.

17

"Guess what?" Mandy asked, out of breath from running to meet me as I turned the corner to school.

"Guess what for me, too," I said.

"What?" Mandy asked.

"I got a baby kitten Saturday. Come see her after school—she's so cute!"

Then I remembered Mandy's guess what.

"What?" I asked her.

"Aunt Betty, remember my rich Aunt Betty? She's going to let me have a swim party at her house on Saturday. You know, a 'let's get ready for summer, school's out' party. You've got to help me, Cassie. Okay?"

"Okay," I said.

I didn't know if Mandy's Aunt Betty was really rich or not, but she sure was richer than anyone else we knew. She lived in a big house up in the Heights. She had a swimming pool, hot tub, dressing rooms, and a sort of recreation room with a kitchen, all in her backyard. Oh, yeah, and a shuffle-board game in one cemented area and a brick barbecue in another.

"We can invite twenty-four kids, and we can start at 1:00 in the afternoon. We can bring stuff to eat for dinner, and dance in the rec room, and we don't have to end the party until 11:00. Isn't it great, Cassie?"

I had to admit, even though I'm not often enthused about parties, that this one sounded pretty good.

During English we started making lists of people we'd invite, and lists of food we wanted to have. Marlow, in his last-week-of-school tieless shirt, handed back some term papers. I got a C- with a note saying how much more he'd expected from me. I guessed that meant I'd end up with a C in English. I'd never had less than a B in English before, and I dreaded taking my report card home this time. I hoped my parents wouldn't get all freaked out about my grades and want me to go to summer school or something.

I put Jason first on my invitation list, and Mandy put Eric first on hers.

We didn't have to do anything for gym the last week of school—just show up and sit around. Mandy and I finished the lists during gym. We ended up with fourteen girls' names and only ten boys.

"Do you think we should keep it more even?" Mandy asked. "Like not invite two of the girls, and maybe invite that creep, Herman?"

"No. I think we should invite people we like. What girls would we leave off, anyway?"

"I don't know. Maybe Sheila. But we couldn't really leave off Sheila and invite Pam. And we couldn't leave off Pam and invite Terri. Besides, I don't really want to leave Sheila out. I like her."

"Yeah, me too. And I don't really want to invite Herman. You know how he always walks up behind girls and pulls their bra straps. He'd be gross at a swim party," I said.

I had a terrible thought, but I tried to put it out of my mind.

We decided not to try to keep things even. So what if we had more girls than boys?

During science, when I was bored, the terrible thought came creeping back into my brain. I'd have to wear a bathing suit in front of all those kids and Jason! How embarrassing— my flat chest and big butt on display. I could wear my extra-large, long sweatshirt over my bathing suit most of the time, but I couldn't swim in that. Maybe I should just not go swimming at the party. No, that would be boring …

"Give her your science book, Cassie," Julia said, poking me in the back.

I looked up. Mrs. Wilson was standing beside me, waiting for my book. She'd been going down each row, collecting books. I fumbled around in my book bag while she looked down at me. I handed her my book. She flipped through the pages, checked the binding, and made a little mark beside my name on her book list, then moved back to Julia.

When I saw Dr. Shipper on Wednesday afternoon, the first thing she asked about was the assignment.

"I got a kitten!" I told her. "Mom would never let us have pets and I always wanted one, and this time she said it was okay."

"Tell me about it, Cassie. Why did she let you have a pet this time, when she always said no before?"

I told her how I'd arranged with the little girl to take the kitten back within two weeks if my mother thought it was too much trouble. And how I arranged with Grammy to bring Tangle with me this summer, and how Robbie and I had set things up so it was easy to clean up after Tangle.

"So, even though you told me you didn't know anything you wanted to have happen for yourself when we talked about the assignment, you had a very strong desire for something, didn't you?"

"Yeah, I did. I just didn't remember it until I saw those little kittens. And then I knew how much I'd always wanted a kitten."

"Why didn't you think of that in here, when I asked you about what you wanted?"

"I don't know," I told her. "I guess I'd just kind of put it out of my mind. I didn't think I could ever have a pet, so I didn't think about it."

"That's part of our task here together, Cassie," Dr. Shipper said, "to get you to know what's going on inside of you, so you can deal with things important to you. You've had a lot of confusing feelings over your experiences with Fred Sloane, and one very natural response to confusing feelings is to try to put them out of your mind. But that doesn't really work, because those feelings show themselves in other ways."

Then Dr. Shipper shocked me by how much she seemed to know about me. She asked me these questions that I think she already knew the answers to.

"Did you take more baths after this man first touched and kissed you?"

"Yeah, all the time. Well, not baths usually, but showers." Then I remembered how I'd taken a scalding hot bath the night that Fred had caught me in his hallway.

"And baths, too," I said.

"Why do you think you took more baths and showers at that time?"

"I guess I felt dirty," I said.

"Did all of that washing make you feel clean?"

"It helped," I told her, "for a while, anyway."

"But it didn't make those feelings go away?"

"No. I guess it didn't, really, 'cause I kept having to take more and more showers."

I didn't say this, but right then I was feeling like I could hardly wait to get home and take a shower, even though I'd taken one in the morning before I went to school.

"Did you wear heavy clothing, even when it was warm out?" she asked.

I nodded, thinking about my jacket. It was hot out right then, but I missed my jacket.

"I have a favorite jacket that I wear all the time. Daddy says I have to stop wearing it because it's summertime almost, and I'll roast to death."

"Do you want to stop wearing it?"

"Kind of. I mean, it is hot, and it looks funny to be wearing a big jacket when it's about ninety-eight degrees in the shade. But I like wearing it, too … It's safe," I said. I didn't even know why I said that.

"Safe from what?"

"From people. From touching and looking," I said.

We talked for a long time about those things, and I ended up confessing that I didn't want anyone at the swim party to see me in a bathing suit, especially Jason. We talked about being embarrassed, and about how probably everyone else going to that party had some of those same feelings, and about trying to like myself.

"What do you like about your body, Cassie?" Dr. Shipper asked.

"It works pretty good," I told her.

"What do you mean?"

"Well, I'm good at soccer, and I like to run, and I'm strong. I can beat my seventeen-year-old cousin at arm wrestling."

"What do you like about the way you look?"

"Not much," I said.

"Choose something," she told me.

"Well … I'm not fat."

"No fair," she told me. "It has to be something you are, not something you aren't."

"Okay. I have good legs," I said. But I didn't really want to say it. It sounded conceited.

The buzzer went off. "Here's your next assignment. Bring me a list of at least ten other things you like about yourself. Anything. I'll see you Monday, before you go to your grandmother's. Right?"

"Right," I said, and left.

All year long I'd been looking forward to going to Grammy's, and now I was beginning to think of all I'd miss. I'd miss Mandy. And I wondered if Jason would still like me when I got back. I might even miss these counseling times.

Friday night Mom and Daddy and Robbie and I all went shopping together. Robbie and I got clothes for the summer. I got three new pairs of shorts and three tops, a pair of sandals and a bathing suit.

Before I went to bed that night I tried on my bathing suit again and stood in front of the mirror. I was not Miss Universe. I tried to see something I liked, so I could put it on the list for Dr. Shipper. I had a flat stomach. I liked that. And my legs were okay. And my arms. I had good arm muscles from volleyball and tetherball. I was kind of surprised to see that I was not exactly as flat-chested as I had been when I stood in front of my mirror a few months ago. Sort of a big butt, though. Average face. Oh well, I thought, it would have to do. I liked my new bathing suit a lot, so that helped.

The party was great. Once I got in the water I forgot about being embarrassed. Eric and Jason and I raced the length of the pool and back. I won.

Later, Julia said to me, "Don't you know you're never supposed to beat a guy at anything if you want him to like you?"

"I just swim faster," I told her.

"But you should pretend you can't," she said.

"I'm not into pretending," I told her. It surprised me, because I never disagreed with Julia about stuff like that. I think it surprised her, too. She just laughed.

We played volleyball and shuffleboard and then we barbecued hot dogs. Later we danced. Some of the other guys asked me to dance, and I did. But all of the slow dances I danced with Jason. We danced real close, and after someone turned the lights down low, he kissed me, more than once. It felt good. Somebody liked me and I liked him. It was easy to kiss him.

"Will you give me your grandmother's telephone number and address before you leave?" he asked. "Maybe I can call you, or even come see you sometime. Would that be okay?"

I said it would. I walked away right then, in search of a pencil and paper. I just left Jason standing there. That probably wasn't too cool. When I came back he was talking to Julia, but as soon as he saw me he came over to meet me. I gave him the slip of paper, and we started dancing again.

Mandy and I spent the night at her aunt's house so we could clean everything up the next day. We talked a long, long time after everyone left. I asked Mandy to come spend a week with me at the beach. She said she would. It was kind of a tradition.

"Eric's going away this summer, too," she told me. "I hope he still likes me when he gets back home."

"He will," I told her. "All of the boys like you, so why should he be any different?"

"They don't either," she said. "Probably more boys like you than like me."

"Me? Nobody likes me but Jason," I said.

"Then why did all of those guys ask you to dance?"

"They wanted someone to dance with, and I was there."

"I can't believe you, Cassie! There were about a hundred girls standing there, but guys kept asking you to dance. I know for a fact Tommy Parson likes you!"

"He does not! He hardly even knows me!" I told her. "The better to like you, my dear," she laughed, throwing her pillow at me.

"Well, what about Jimmy Morland? Everyone knows he likes you!" I yelled, and threw the pillow back at her.

We went through the whole list of guys at our school, who liked who and who they didn't, and who liked them. Later I thought about Mandy saying that probably more guys liked me than liked her. I couldn't believe I would ever be as popular as Mandy. Maybe I was more popular than I thought, though. A lot of guys did ask me to dance. I danced more than Julia did. When I realized that, it surprised me.

Just as I was drifting off to sleep, Mandy said, "What's it like to kiss Jason?"

"I like it."

"Can you feel his braces?"

"No—just his lips. What's it like kissing Eric?"

"Heaven," she said.

I threw my pillow at her again, and we started a real pillow fight this time, using all four of the big down pillows in the frilly guest room where we were supposed to be sleeping. The strange thing about a pillow fight at Mandy's aunt's house was that no one even heard because the house was so big. Mandy's aunt slept upstairs at one end of the house, and we were downstairs at the other.

In the morning, after we finished our clean-up job, Mandy's aunt drove us to Mandy's. Later we walked back to my house. "We have to go the long way," I told her.

"Why?"

"I don't want to walk past the Sloanes' house."

"Why not, though? Do you think they'd come after you if they saw you?"

"No. I just don't ever want to see them again," I said.

"You sure used to like them," she reminded me.

"Things change."

Even going the long way, though, when we reached the corner of Fairview and Main, Tina and Dorian were there, Dorian on his tricycle and Tina standing on the back. I knew they weren't supposed to be there. Angie never let them go down to Main Street. I hadn't wanted to see them, but once I did, I liked them. I couldn't help that.

"Hi, Tina. Hi, Dorian," I said.

They just watched us. They didn't say anything.

"You're not supposed to be up here by this busy street," I said. "You'd better go home."

"You're not a nice girl," Dorian said to me.

I felt tears sting my eyes. "Get on home, Dorian," I said. He just sat there on his tricycle.

"Go for it, you little brat!" Mandy yelled, running at him. He pedaled toward home as fast as he could go, with Tina clinging to his back.

Summer was the way I wanted it to be—quiet and peaceful and safe, with lots of swimming and lots of sun. I was alone a lot, I mean, as far as friends and stuff, but I really didn't mind. Once Mandy came and stayed with us for five days. And Lisa came down every weekend. Mom and Daddy, too, came nearly every Sunday. Mostly, though, it was me and Robbie and Tangle and Grammy.

My birthday was August 20, and Mom and Daddy drove down that evening to help me celebrate. We roasted hot dogs over a fire on the beach, and Daddy and I raced from the fire ring to the lifeguard station. I almost beat him! I couldn't believe it. He made a big deal about how my legs were twice as long as they had been in June, and everyone made a big deal about how I was a teenager.

Later, we sat around the fire and roasted marshmallows.

Robbie fell asleep on Mom's lap. Grammy wrapped a beach towel around him and walked him, still sleeping, back home.

We watched the fire for a while, then Daddy said, "Remember how Angie Sloane said you were no different than the others?"

"Yeah, I do," I told him. "I still wonder about that sometimes."

"Apparently what Trudy told us about men following a certain pattern, going after girls of a certain age, was true for Fred," Mom said.

"What do you mean?" I asked.

"It seems he'd been pulling the same thing with his boss's daughter that he'd been pulling with you," Daddy said.

"Carmen?" I asked. "Do you mean Carmen?"

"I guess that's her name. She's twelve. Mr. Casteneda's only daughter. Do you know her?"

"Yeah. She was in my gym class last year. We played soccer together."

"What a coincidence," Mom said.

"Anyway," Daddy said, "the daughter had been doing some work at the muffler shop during the summer. You know, addressing envelopes for ads, running errands, that kind of thing. Well, one day last week, Mr. Casteneda stuck his head out of his office just in time to see Sloane standing behind Carmen with his hand inside her blouse. He went nuts. He picked up a tire iron and chased Sloane out of the shop and down the street, yelling all kinds of things at him in Spanish. The cops came and hauled them both in."

"What about Carmen?" I asked.

"Your friend Sergeant Conrad took Carmen with her, in that unmarked car she drives. It was the most excitement downtown Hamilton Heights has had since the American Legion Bicentennial Parade."

I felt strange. The Fred Sloane stuff had been part of a different world since I came to the beach. Even though I thought about it sometimes, I thought about it from a distance. Now it was up close again.

"Did they keep Fred and Mr. Casteneda in jail?" I asked. I was glad Daddy hadn't gotten so violent with Fred that he had to go to jail!

"They released Mr. Casteneda that evening, but they kept Sloane overnight. I talked with Johnny—you know, the other guy who works at the shop. He told me that Angie wouldn't come to bail Fred out that night. She made him wait until morning before she came with the bail money."

I put two marshmallows on a stick and held them in the fire. I liked them burned on the outside and soupy on the inside.

Mom said, "I heard from their neighbor, Mrs. Graves, that Angie had all of Fred's things sitting in boxes on the front lawn when he got home the next morning, and that even though she'd bailed him out, she wouldn't drive him home. He had to take the bus and then walk the rest of the way. Mrs. Graves hasn't seen Fred around there since that day."

I wondered why Angie had believed what happened with Carmen but she hadn't believed me.

"I'm glad he's gone," Mom said. "I feel sorry for Angie and the children, but they're probably better off without him anyway."

I remembered how Fred had comforted Tina that night she'd been awakened by a bad dream. I didn't know if they were better off without him or not. I thought about how Robbie told me that Tina and Dorian both kissed with their tongues, and I wondered about what might happen when Tina got to be twelve. There was still a lot that confused me.

"Let's walk back and cut the birthday cake," Mom said, getting up and shaking out her towel. "Do you still have room for cake after all those marshmallows and hot dogs?" she asked.

"Is it chocolate?"

"Of course. The birthday girl's favorite flavor. Right?"

"If it's chocolate, I have room," I said.

I wanted to race Daddy back to Grammy's, but he said he was too full. I think he was afraid I might beat him. We ate cake and played Uno until about 11:00.

As Mom and Dad were leaving, Mom said to me, "Oh, I almost forgot. We got a notice about some kind of registration/orientation day at your school on September 2nd. You'll have to come home for that."

Telling

"But school doesn't even start until the 16th," I whined.

"September 2nd is much too early for Cassie to go home," Grammy said, in her most authoritative voice.

"Calm down," Daddy laughed. "We'll bring her back in the evening after she registers, so she can finish out her visit with you here."

Mandy was banging on my door early in the morning on registration day.

"Let me in. I know you're in there."

I ran and threw open the door. She looked great. I'd missed her a lot, and maybe didn't even know it until I saw her again. She walked straight to the refrigerator, removed a dish of leftover beans, helped herself to a couple of slices of bread, made herself a baked bean sandwich, and then led the way back to my room. She told me she didn't know if she still liked Eric or not.

"So much for love," I teased her.

"Do you still like Jason?"

"I think so," I said. "I haven't seen him for a long time, though."

"Didn't you see him at all this summer?" she asked. I shook my head.

"But he called you, didn't he?"

"No," I told her. "But look." I went to my suitcase and got out the folder of cartoons he'd sent to me while I was at the beach.

"There must be a hundred of those things," she said.

"Seventy-one," I told her. "Almost two a day."

"Wow!" she sighed.

When we got ready to leave for school, Mandy convinced me to put on some of her lipstick. It felt strange. I thought about what I'd learned from Dr. Shipper, about figuring out what I wanted to do. I wiped it off, then put some on again. I decided to wear it. I kind of liked the way it looked.

"You look so good, Cassie," Mandy said. "I wish I had your tan!"

I looked in the mirror. I did look pretty good. My hair

was bleached from the sun, and, it's true, I had a great tan. There was no longer a choice between an undershirt and a bra—I was now definitely a bra wearer.

Jason met us at the corner, before we got to the front of the school. We both smiled, but neither of us knew what to say. Jason was taller, and he was just wearing a retainer instead of all those braces he'd had the last time I'd seen him.

"You look different," I told him.

"You, too," he said. Then he made one of his Jason-style quick exits. He was smiling, and I could tell he still liked me. The seventh graders looked small, and they acted like a bunch of babies. I was glad to be in the eighth grade. There was a lot of talk from the counselor and vice-principal about this being our last year before we'd enter Hamilton High School, and how important it was for us to get prepared for ninth grade. It was fun seeing everyone at orientation, but I was glad to get back to Grammy's that night.

In the morning we went to the beach about 11:00, as soon as the fog burned off and the sun came out. That's how we always did. We carried lunch and drinks and Tangle, all in Grammy's covered picnic basket. And we always brought tuna for Tangle. That way she never wandered very far away.

Early in the afternoon, Grammy and Robbie and Tangle went back home, but I stayed later. It was my favorite time of day, after the crowd was gone, and the tide was far out. Then I watched starfish and sea anemones and all kinds of little creatures in the tide pools.

It intrigues me how all of them managed to get along— how a starfish could even lose an arm and then grow it back. And I thought about how people could lose things, and feel empty, and then start to feel okay.

I thought about Fred and Angie, and my friends at school. I thought about Jason, too, and my parents. I thought about stuff that scared me, like what if there was a war and the whole world was blown up—or what if Tangle went too far from home and got run over by a car—or what if I was real ugly when I grew up.

Telling

I ran into the water and swam out past where the waves were breaking. I was floating on my back out in the water, looking up at the sky. The sun was warm on the front of my body, and the water was cool and bracing and strong under my back. The clouds were pure white, billowy, and the sky was blue and clear. I heard the sounds of gulls overhead, and voices from a distant volleyball game. I was being gently rocked by ocean rhythms. I know it sounds corny, but it was like being rocked in the arms of God, and I knew I belonged to it all.

EPILOGUE

That all happened about five years ago. I hardly ever think about it anymore, unless there's some kind of reminder. Like, I never ride the Pirates of the Caribbean at Disneyland without remembering the Sloane family. And once, at the movies, when my boyfriend kissed me, the taste of popcorn on his mouth sent me right back to the time of Fred Sloane.

What started me thinking about it this time was a letter I got from Angie last week. I never saw Angie again, after her time in our front yard. Mrs. Graves told me that Angie and the kids went back to Minnesota to live with her parents, and that Fred got a job working on a pipeline in Alaska.

Anyway, last week in our mailbox, along with the proofs for my senior pictures, was a letter to me—with no return address. It said:

Dear Cassie,
I hardly know how to say this, so I'll just start. I've become a member of Alcoholics Anonymous, which is a long story, but one of the steps A.A. members must take is to make a list of all the persons we've harmed and to make direct amends whenever possible. You're on my list of people I've harmed.
I'm sorry I accused you of lying and attacked you. I know you trusted me and looked up to me, and I'm sure I hurt you. I was trying to believe in Fred, and the biggest liar of all was me, lying to myself. Please forgive me.
I hope all is going well for you.
Sincerely, Angie

I cried when I read it. I never really held any grudge against Angie. But I do feel better about her now than before she wrote. Maybe in some hidden corner of myself there was an Angie spot that was dark and murky, and now there's a little more light there.

I'm different now. I still like to play soccer, and get silly with Mandy, and pig out on Rice Krispies treats. But when I was twelve I hardly ever thought about the future, or what I would do with my life. Now I think about those things all the time. I want to make everything fit.

I think about how important love is, and a family, and how I want a career. Right now I think I'll major in psychology and maybe work for the sheriff's department, like Connie. Or maybe I'll have my own practice, like Dr. Shipper. Anyway, I want to do something important—something that helps people. And for sure I always want to remember to take time out to float on my back in the ocean, and look up at the blue, blue sky, and know that I'm a part of it all.

ABOUT THE AUTHOR

In addition to Telling, Marilyn Reynolds is the author of ten other books of realistic teen fiction: Eddie's Choice, Shut Up, No More Sad Goodbyes, Love Rules, If You Loved Me, But What About Me?, Beyond Dreams, Baby Help, Too Soon for Jeff and Detour for Emmy, all part of the popular True-to-Life Series from Hamilton High. Reynolds is also the author of a book for educators, *I Won't Read and You Can't Make Me: Reaching Reluctant Teen Readers.* Reynolds has a variety of published personal essays to her credit, and was nominated for the ABC Afterschool Special teleplay of Too Soon for Jeff.

Reynolds worked with reluctant learners and teens in crises at a southern California alternative high school for more than two decades. She remains actively involved in education through author presentations to middle and high school students ranging from struggling readers to highly motivated writers who are interested in developing work for possible publication. She also presents staff development workshops for educators and is often a guest speaker for programs and organizations that serve teens, parents, teachers, and writers.

Reynolds lives in Sacramento where she enjoys neighborhood walks, visits with friends and family, movies and dinner out, and the luxury of reading at odd hours of the day and night.

ABOUT THE TYPE

This book was set in Bembo, a typeface based on an old-style Roman face that was used for Cardinal Bembo's tract *De Aetna* in 1495. Bembo was cut by Francisco Griffo in the early sixteenth century. The Lanston Monotype Company of Philadelphia brought the well-proportioned letterforms of Bembo to the United States in the 1930s.

CPSIA information can be obtained
at www.ICGtesting.com
Printed in the USA
FSHW011039090919
61831FS